There's No Such Thing As Ghosts!

Best wishes,

Pam Keead

There's No Such Thing As Ghosts!

Pam Keevil

Matador
5 Weir Road
Kibworth Beauchamp
Leicester LE8 0LQ, UK
Tel: 0116 279 2299
Fax: 0116 279 2277
Email: books@troubador.co.uk
Web: www.troubador.co.uk/matador

ISBN 978 1848764 774

British Library Cataloguing in Publication Data.
A catalogue record for this book is available from the British Library.

All characters are fictitious and any resemblance to people living or dead is entirely
co incidental. The details about Corinium that are historically correct are in the
Footnotes at the back of the book.

Typeset in 12pt Palatino by Troubador Publishing Ltd, Leicester, UK

Matador is an imprint of Troubador Publishing Ltd

Printed in Great Britain by the MPG Books Group, Bodmin and King's Lynn

Dedicated to the children, parents, staff and Governors
of Cirencester Junior School 1/9/1971-31/8/2010

With thanks to the staff at the Corinium Museum for
their help.

CONTENTS

CHAPTER ONE

8.45 am; the present day, Thursday September 3rd

"If you ever go to the loo on your own, Annie the ghost will get you!" Laura Glade aimed a well timed push at the younger child's back and then ran off across the school field, her long blonde hair streaming behind her. As she ran, she deliberately swung her bag from side to side, laughing and giggling and trying to hit any other passing child that was smaller than her. Shelley, her best friend followed, plodding as fast as she could and the two disappeared around the corner of the school and onto the playground. Donna stopped still until they were out of sight then increased her pace until she drew level with the two younger children. They were walking slowly and very reluctantly towards the school gate. One of them looked up at Donna, lip trembling and eyes filled with tears.

"There's no such thing as ghosts," Donna whispered, pushing back a stray wisp of curly brown hair that was desperately trying to escape from its tight hair band.

"How do you know?" The lip wobbled even more.

"My granddad's the caretaker and he's always here late at night and he's never seen anything," Donna answered defiantly. They smiled weakly. "Now go on, run ahead," she continued, "You don't want to be late on the first day of school do you?"

As they hurried off, Donna hung back. One of her football mates would arrive soon and they could walk in together. Somehow, Laura and Shelley never picked on her in front of them. She waited. No one came. The insistent clanging of the first bell rang out over the field. Sighing, she slung her school bag over her shoulder and continued across the field, her feet squelching in the wet grass.

"Donna…wait! Wait for me…" Donna turned to see Sam running towards her, his hands and knees covered in dirt and a streak of mud smeared across his face. "Guess what?" he panted.

"What?"

"Guess what I've found?" But he didn't wait for her to reply. "I've found Annie!" The second bell rang.

"Annie is a story, you numnut! Now come on or we'll be late!"

"But I have found her. Look at this." He pulled a dirty tissue from his pocket and carefully opened it up. Inside was a circle of metal. One end was flattened and there were two holes, like eyes. He spat on it and rubbed it hard. The metal had a faint greenish yellow tinge.

"Give it here." Donna snatched it for a closer look. "You dummy, it looks like gold. Where did

3

you find it?"

"It belongs to Annie!" Sam announced with pride. "I'll show you after school today, if you like, but you must promise never, never, ever tell anyone." He wrapped it up in the tissue and put it back in his pocket.

"If this is some stupid game, Sam, watch out. I am not into it."

"It's not, you'll see. Meet me this afternoon! I've found Annie!" he announced again triumphantly and ran off ahead of Donna, leaving her to chase after him. She slipped into the playground unnoticed, just as the third bell rang and joined the back of the line behind him. Together they waited quietly whilst Mrs Jones went up and down the line checking for correct school uniform. She stopped in front of Sam and folded her arms. Donna held her breath, wondering what she would say. "Why are you already in such a mess this morning?" the shrill voice pierced the September air. "Have you been playing on that slope?"

4

"No." There was a pause whilst Sam studied his feet, "...er..I fell over." Donna stepped quickly out of the line to stand beside him.

"It's true, Mrs Jones. I saw him so I helped him up and then we walked to school together." Donna, took off her thick glasses and rubbed them on her sweatshirt, screwing up her face in concentration.

There was a long pause as Mrs Jones looked from one to the other. Donna stood as still as a statue. Any squirming and Mrs Jones would suspect them. A voice from a nearby classroom drifted out of an open window, "Find your seats everyone." Still Mrs Jones stared at both of them. Funny, thought Donna, she'd never noticed before how the wind couldn't move the iron like structure that was Mrs Jones' hair. It must be held in place with glue.

"Very well. But be more careful in future. You're in my class now and remember what everyone calls me!" and she scuttled towards the front of the line.

Sam turned round to face Donna, "What do

they call her?"

"The dragon!"

"Why?"

"Because she's fierce!"

Sam nodded, "Thanks, Moo-cow."

"No talking at the back there." Mrs Jones led the way into the school for another year. But this time Donna was determined it would be different.

As everyone else trooped into the classroom, Donna hung back by the door trying to avoid the usual scrum of finding a place to sit on the first day of term, but Mrs Jones had already put name cards on each of the desks. Out of the corner of her eye, she saw Laura pouting because she was not sitting with her best friend, Shelley. Then Donna saw her deliberately reach out and switch names with Liam. Triumphantly, she plonked herself down in the desk next to Shelley and stared around her, defying anyone to complain. But no one else had noticed. Donna found her desk at the front and slipped into the seat next to Sam, casting one last look behind her. Laura noticed, nudged Shelley and pointed at Donna. They both giggled. "Why are you two sitting together?" Mrs Jones looked up from the register.

"Our names were here, Mrs Jones," Laura explained sweetly. "Would you like us to move?"

"Are you sure?" Mrs Jones looked uncomfortable for a moment.

"They were here, weren't they Shell?"

"Yeah, that's right."

Mrs Jones paused and looked from one to the other but Laura was a master at pretending to be innocent. "Very well, but if you two spend more time talking than working you will be moved. Do you understand?"

"Of course, Mrs Jones." Laura stared straight at Donna, as if daring her to say something but Donna quickly turned back to face the front. She'd better not do anything this early in the term to draw Laura's attention to her. Her plan of action this year was to keep out of Laura's way as much as possible and then perhaps she would get bored and find someone else to pick on. At least that was what Donna hoped as she drew a margin and filled in the date on a brand new page of a new book.

Break time came eventually. The cloakroom was quiet as Donna opened her bag to search for her lunch box. "Don't you dare say anything!" Laura appeared as if from nowhere, grabbed hold of Donna's arm and dug her nails into the flesh. Donna winced and pulled her arm away as quickly as she could.

"What about?"

"Me and Shell sitting together. I know you saw me switch names, but you've been warned."

"Yeah," Shelley added.

"Warned about what?"Mrs Jones rounded the corner into the cloakroom, on her way to the staff room.

"Nothing, Mrs Jones, just talking," Laura smiled sweetly.

"Donna? Is that right?"

Donna nodded, her hand rubbing her wrist.

"Is there anything wrong with your wrist?"

"No, Mrs Jones, just an itch," Donna scratched at her arm then hurriedly pulled her sweatshirt sleeve down over the red marks. Mrs Jones looked from one to the other, slowly,

"Very well, but you should all be outside now."

Avoiding Mrs Jones' piercing glare, Donna grabbed an apple from her bag and followed Laura and Shelley outside. She'd join in with the game of football as usual then they'd leave her alone.

She was just about to take the throw, carefully watching for who was in a space when she overheard Mr Shah talking to two Y5 pupils. He was standing by the goal and watching the game.

"Sir, someone says there's this girl, Annie, who fell out of the school over there," the blonde one pointed to the blocked up window that always reminded Donna of a doorway.

"Yes and if you spin round twice in the toilets

and look in the mirror you can see her," the other added, her eyes sparkling with the thought. Donna threw the ball and called out to Matthew to take her place. She sidled closer to hear more.

"It's even better if you hold your collar, stand on one leg, close one eye and eat a banana at the same time," added Mr Shah, a smile spreading across his face.

"Really?"

"Only if there's a 'z ' in the month!" he continued. The two girls looked at each other then realised he was teasing.

"Oh Sir. Go on – tell us the truth!"

"There never has been an 'Annie'. The room behind that door is just a store room with a water tank in it. Now off you go and don't listen to any more silly tales. The bell will go any minute."

Donna stepped forward, "Mr Shah, what do you know about the stories of Annie? Is any of it true?" Somehow Donna had to find out the truth or Sam might get himself into trouble again with his crazy ideas.

"I doubt it. That story has been going round for years. If there was any truth in it, there would be information in the school log books." Donna must have looked puzzled as Mr Shah added, "Until a few years ago, every school had to keep a log book of events that had happened. There is absolutely nothing about an 'Annie' or anyone else – and remember, there's no such thing as ghosts!"

"Thanks, sir." Donna ran back to join the football game, quickly taking a pass from Joe and chipping it into the net just as the bell rang. She made her way to the class line. So what had Sam found? The end of school couldn't come quick enough.

The third bell rang and everyone was silent. Mrs Jones bustled forward with her list. "Now, all these people will be with me in my maths group," and she proceeded to read out a list of names. Donna listened. Laura's name was called out but not hers. Her heart began to pound. Another list was read out and that included Shelley. Donna allowed herself a small smile. "I don't know what is so funny, Donna. We are all very disappointed in your maths last year. You should be in my top maths group but as you did not work hard last year, you will have to go down a group."

Donna bit her lip but said nothing. How could anyone work with Laura always ready to pinch or punch or poke at you whenever the teacher's back was turned. "I'm sure if you work hard, you can get back into the top set," Mrs Jones added brightly. That, thought Donna was exactly what she was not going to do. She'd never be so stupid that she'd have to go down into Shelley's group. They still couldn't do their two times table. But she had no intention of going into the same group as Laura, again. Being in her class was bad enough and the thought of just one Laura free hour every day was bliss. She'd make sure she stayed right where she was, even if it meant making mistakes from time to time.

The day dragged on. It was silent reading at the

end of the day when the class phone rang. Shelley jumped up, as it was her turn to answer it. "Class 6J. How can I help you?"

She listened for a while. "Mrs Jones, Sam's mum says he has to come home now, he's got a dentist's appointment."

"Very well, Sam, get your things," Mrs Jones announced without looking up from her reading group.

"Tomorrow, at the bridge. Ok?" he muttered to Donna as he was putting away his books. She nodded.

"Sam's departure does not mean a general invitation to talk." Mrs Jones called out but she carried on with hearing her group read and did not look up.

"This secret had better be a good one!" Donna hissed.

"It is, see you," he slung his book bag over his back and hurried out.

"I said no talking!" This time Mrs Jones did

look up. "Really Donna, what has got into you this term?" Donna bent her head over her book and said nothing. Tomorrow she would find out exactly what Sam was up to and it had better be good.

5.30pm; the same day

"Don't you dare speak to me like that!" Paul Glade thundered as Laura turned her back on him, and flounced up the stairs.

She closed her bedroom door with a deliberate bang and wedged the door underneath the handle. "Cow," she muttered, "cow, cow, cow!" louder and louder but not loud enough that the remaining members of the family down stairs could hear. She would not eat the disgusting food that Sarah had prepared. She wished her dad had never met her. It was so much better when they were on their own. She punched the pillow as she remembered the long evenings, curled up with her father on the sofa, eating pizza and watching the TV and teasing Jamie, her pain of a brother. But now that Sarah had moved in, nothing was the same and soon there would be a baby. Had anyone asked her or Jamie if they wanted another brother or sister?

Downstairs the phone rang shrilly. It was answered almost immediately. "Councillor Paul Glade here." Usually Laura didn't take any notice, but this time something in the excited way her father answered the phone made her creep to the top of the stair and listen . "That is fantastic news!"

Laura listened more carefully. She could just see her father; his glasses perched on the top of his curly grey hair, stretched out in his leather office chair. "This is just what we need. It'll be a chance to get rid of some scrubby bit of land and make shed-loads of money for the Young Children's group!" He fell silent again. "So Waste.com have finally agreed to build their new recycling unit here." He paused and Laura could hear him laughing. "That might shut up the newly elected

Green representative and stop her bleating on in her woolly hatted way about recycling." There was another pause, "Of course we'll get the press onto it right away. Thanks for letting me know," and he slammed the phone down.

Laura sprang back into her room, but not before she had heard him mutter under his breath, "The new Mayor Paul Glade announces yet another first for the town!" Laura gently closed her bedroom door. This was obviously very important to her father. She made a mental note to remember this for the future then switched on her phone to check for messages from Shelley.

Much later, there was a knock at the door. "I'll make you a sandwich if you like, Laura?" Sarah whispered.

"I'm not hungry."

"Well if you feel like coming down at any time, I can easily make you something."

"Don't bother," replied Laura as the footsteps moved downstairs, but so quietly that no one could hear. Oh why couldn't everything be back the way she had liked it! There was another tap at the door, "Go away!"

"It's only me. Let me in,"Jamie pleaded.

Laura went to the door and pulled away the chair. Jamie came and sat down beside her on her shiny blue satin bed. "Why are you crying? Has there been another row?"

"I'm not crying," Laura insisted.

"Yes you are. Your nose is wet or is it snot?" Jamie peered at her from underneath his long black fringe.

"You're disgusting." But she punched his arm just the same and smiled weakly.

"Why don't you come down? Sarah's made chocolate cake." Jamie's thoughts were never far from food or computer games.

"I liked it the way we were… why did she have to come and spoil everything…?" Laura punched at the pillow again.

"Well we can't do anything about it. Sarah is

here and dad is happy. Why don't you just give her a chance? If she makes dad happy that's good enough for me." He rubbed Laura's hair.

"Don't!" she twisted away from his grasp.

"Sorry. Look, come down in a little while and we can play the new game that I borrowed from Dan. It needs two people." He stood up to go. "Laura?"

"I might." The door closed behind him. Laura punched the pillow yet again. She should be the one to make her dad happy, not Sarah.

There was another knock at her door. "Laura!" Paul Glade stood outside. "I'm sorry you are upset. But I will not have Sarah spoken to in that way. I'm sure we can work something out…" he faltered. "Listen, I'm sorry I shouted. I've got a big project on at work and I'm probably a bit stressed out. What if I made it up to you? I know you need a new phone. Is there one you like? What about that new black one that's advertised on TV?" Laura sat up. A smile crept across her face.

"Thanks, dad. Perhaps I will be down in a minute." That new phone would make everyone at school jealous. Perhaps she could even manage a slice of chocolate cake after all!

Mid day; 160 AD

"You promised!" screamed Aurea as she clutched her stomach, which swelled uncomfortably beneath the metal slave belt.

"Quiet, girl" Senator Gaius looked nervously round the shadowy room. "There are people downstairs in the kitchen. No one must know anything about this."

"If anything happens to me or our baby, everything that you have told me about your schemes will reach the ears of Marcus Aurelius. How do you think the Emperor would feel if he knew his son and you, his most trusted senator were plotting to overthrow him?" Gaius looked around again. A bead of sweat stood out on his forehead in the stifling midday air. Aurea waited, enjoying his discomfort.

"You cannot let me stay here. I know too much and you do not have the courage to order my death, even if it does look like an accident! You are far too weak and no one will take my child from me and leave him to his fate." There was another long pause, "I would need at least twenty thousand sesterces to keep quiet," Aurea continued.

"Is that all?"

"Each year, of course!"

"That's madness!"

"Then what will you do with me?" Aurea sat on the end of the small bench by the window and gazed at the courtyard below. She could hear Gaius pacing up and down and she knew he would be running his hands through his grey hair in exasperation. She sat absolutely still.

"I have an idea…" he came and sat on the

window ledge beside her. "My brother has recently gone to Corinium as administrator of the region. He would be happy to have a trustworthy slave in that place. I could say you were married to a dead gladiator who had recently won his freedom and I was doing him a favour." He paused, "Yes, that is what will happen!"

"Where is Corinium?" Aurea demanded, still staring down into the courtyard.

"Britannia. You will be safe there, and the baby."

Aurea thought hard. "I will not go to that distant place," she paused, "as a slave and neither will your child be brought up as a slave." She turned towards him and a smile crept across her face. "Remember, I know all your schemes!" She yawned and stretched out her arms, "But I am very good at keeping a secret. Instead of a slave, let me go as a servant for his wife but with enough money to keep our child safe should anything happen to me." She turned away and looked out onto the courtyard below. No one moved in the hot dry mid day sun and not a sound could be heard. She lowered her voice to a whisper, "Then I want some jewels, a fur, and enough clothes for myself and the baby."

"You drive a hard bargain."

Aurea turned back to face him and smiled again, but when she spoke, her voice was cold and calculating, "What would be the effect on your own wife and children to realise that their father was a liar and a cheat as well as a traitor? I cannot believe that your wife would accept a life of banishment and sit back and watch as her daughters were forced to marry mere merchants or even farmers! Perhaps there could be an accident and she would be left a widow. Better a widow than a traitor's wife!"

Aurea knew Gaius was beaten. A whiff of scandal like this would ruin his political career and the future of his family.

"Very well. But you leave tonight. You will stay

with my father until I get the money. There is a ship to Britannia next week." Aurea got up from her seat by the window.

"There is one more thing. Undo this belt." She spat the words out as if they were poison. "Treasured and valued servants do not wear slave belts. Release me!" If she could not marry a rich man, she could at least be granted her freedom. Gaius nodded then leaned closer and undid the metal belt which fell to the floor with a clang.

"Now go. You have what you want."

"Thank you. I will look after the baby well. He will be a great soldier."

"Take this." Gaius removed a gold amulet from his wrist. It was in the shape of a snake with a flattened head and emerald eyes. He held it out to Aurea. " It will bring you luck."

Aurea slipped the bangle onto her wrist. "Now wait here."

Gaius went out of the room and Aurea could

hear hushed voices. He quickly returned with one of his soldiers. "Maximus will accompany you to my father's house. You will be safe with him until it is time to leave. " Aurea picked up her cloak and a small bag.

"And what about the money and the furs, clothes and jewels – all the things you promised me?"

"They will be with you before you leave." Aurea pulled the cloak over her head as if to disguise herself and hurried down the staircase to the waiting horses. Within a week, she was on a ship for Britannia, never to return.

9.00pm; the same day

All was quiet as the caretaker, Tom Stephens locked the office door and crossed the hall, turning off the lights as he went. Half way across the hall, he stopped and listened. There was a faint banging sound, like a window. He followed the sound and flung open the music room door. All the windows were closed. Then he noticed a bag on the floor. He picked the bag up and put it onto the bench where it toppled onto the floor again with a slight thump. He moved the bag to the side of the room and went out. As he set the alarm by the staff entrance and finally closed the door for the night, the mist coming up from the river and cloaking the school field wreathed around the bell tower like a sinuous arm.

This is the window that everyone says Annie fell from and

there is a secret room behind here.

Donna

CHAPTER TWO

8.40 am; the present day, Friday September 4th

A thin finger of mist wreathed around the trees along the pathway that led down from the estate onto the school field. Donna pulled her sweatshirt sleeves over her hands and hugged her bag closer to her as she shivered in the damp early September air.

"Boo. Bet that scared you." Sam jumped out from the undergrowth and stood in front of her on the path. His hands and knees were covered in rusty wet soil and he held up a piece of stone triumphantly. "Look – an arrow head!"

"It's a pointed stone, dummy."

"And what about this?" Sam pulled out a piece of orangey red pottery from his pocket. "I bet this is from a Roman pot!"

"Why should it be? "Donna asked.

"'Cause this place is crawling with things. All I need to do is to find some and it'll be treasure trove or I could be famous. I've got loads of things in my den. Do you want a look?" and he dived back into the hedge. "Don't tell anyone," he hissed as a crowd of buggy pushing mothers with small children rounded the corner at the top of the slope and headed towards Donna and he disappeared.

Donna heaved a sigh and waited for the crowd to go past. But just as she was about to follow, the distant sound of a bell could be heard across the field. "Sam. The bell. Come on!" she shouted then turned it into a strangled cough as a late mother dragged her protesting child down the slope and past where Donna was standing.

A second bell sounded. What if Sam hadn't heard? He was always in trouble. Donna hesitated.

The third bell sounded. They were now late so she might as well find out why Sam was acting so strangely. Donna quickly glanced round. There was no one in sight. She stepped off the path into the forbidden territory of brambles, hedges, half-fallen trees and the stream which wound its way through the scrubland. This was private land with the occasional sign threatening any trespassers with prosecution and so entry was strictly forbidden. Peering this way and that she plunged deeper into the undergrowth. Brambles clutched at her jumper and caught in her hair but still she continued deeper into the woodland.

Suddenly Donna stopped and listened. A faint rustling sound made her glance towards a pile of bracken fronds that moved suspiciously. Lifting one aside she saw Sam bent over a pile of stones and bits. "This is where I found her bracelet!" Donna must have looked puzzled. "The bracelet belongs to Annie," he explained patiently.

"Annie is a made up story to scare the little

kids. There has never been an Annie and there never will be." Donna glanced at her watch. School had already started. "Look, let's come back later and you can tell me everything."

"And will you help me explore?" Sam wrapped the bracelet in his sweatshirt which he stuffed at the bottom of his bag.

"Ok, but what's this bracelet got to do with the story of Annie?"

"Tell you later!"

Together they raced across the damp field and reached the gate just as Tom, the caretaker was about to lock the gate. "You're cutting it a bit fine this morning and it's only the second day of term. You haven't been messing around, have you?"

"No, Grandad, Mum says we're not in our routine yet. " Donna smiled and nudged Sam hard.

"I don't think your mother would know what a routine is; still, as long as you're here now but don't be late again or you'll cop it from me as well as school." He finished locking the gates and put the keys safely in his pocket.

"Sorry Grandad," Donna muttered.

"You don't have to say sorry to me. Whose class are you in?"

"Mrs Jones."

"Well run along. From what I've heard she's in a right old mood this morning."

"Why did you nudge me like that?" Sam hissed as they ran across the playground.

"No one minds at the start of term if we're a bit late. Every one knows that," Donna giggled, "So just pretend you overslept!"

They scuttled down the corridor and came to a halt outside Mrs Jones's class, wondering who was going to be brave enough to open the door. "Let me do the talking," Donna insisted as she pushed the door slowly open and she and Sam crept inside. Mrs Jones swung round, book in her hand, open at the page of instructions she had been reading to her class. Only Laura's voice broke the silence,

"Yeah and my dad's getting me that new

phone, the one advertised on TV." But even her voice faded away as the whole class stopped what they were doing and stared at Sam and Donna.

"You are both late. This is not a good start to the term and what on earth have you got over your hands?" Mrs Jones peered at Sam.

"Looks like poo to me…"Matthew sniggered

"Thank you Mathew, when I need a class clown, you may apply for the post."

"Sam dropped his dinner money and it rolled into the ditch…" Donna began, "…and he overslept," she added hurriedly.

"But I have sandwiches. Ouch!"

A sharp kick from Donna stopped him as she continued in a loud voice, " then Sam realised he had sandwiches so he doesn't need any money and we can try and find it after school. Isn't that right Sam?" Donna looked at him hard at the same time as she gave him another sharp kick on the ankle.

This time Sam understood, "Er that's right, Mrs Jones, sorry."

Mrs Jones looked from one to the other. "Next time, spare me the stories and just admit you are late. Now go to your places and –" she glared at Laura, "if that phone ever comes into school I will confiscate it for such a long time that it will no longer be in fashion, it will be a museum piece."

As Donna slipped into her seat, she felt a piece of paper hit her on the back of the head and there was a stifled laugh from Laura and Shelley. Donna picked it up and opened it. "Donna and Sam 4 ever" it read. She sighed, tired of the stupidity of Laura and Shelley. She'd keep out of their way. They would soon find someone else to laugh at. Donna opened her book. Perhaps Sam had found something special after all. That might teach those two a lesson and Donna allowed herself a few minutes to daydream of a Shelley and Laura free world – a world where people might take notice of her, Donna, for once.

The school day dragged past as everyone struggled with complex sentences, long multiplication and the tedious details of science. Why did anyone want to set up experiments to grow cress? It only needed water and a bit of old flannel. She'd grown cress heads with her Grandad ages ago. But she went through the motions of completing the worksheet.

2.30pm the same day

It was not until the class were let out onto the games field that Donna had a chance to talk to Sam. She sidled forwards to where Sam was standing. She nudged his elbow, but before she could say anything, Mr Andrews looked up from the bag of rugby balls that were spilling everywhere and spotted her.

"Donna just the person, here, take this ball and go with Sam, Jake, Aaliyah, Kirwan and Laura and set up passing shots over there." He waved to the far corner of the field and threw her a ball which

Donna caught expertly. Then she turned and ran with her group, passing the ball easily to Sam and trying to ignore the sullen face of Laura who had been split up from Shelley.

It was during a drinks stop when Mr Andrews was explaining passes and everyone else was stretched out on the grass daydreaming, that Donna noticed a large black car that drove down onto the edge of the field and purred to a halt. Three men got out and were met by the Head teacher, Mrs Jarvis, who had followed them down Cuss's Lane on foot.

"That's my dad. What's he doing here?" Laura spoke aloud and all the children turned to watch the four in deep conversation.

Suddenly Mrs Jarvis broke away from the group and waved at the children, before hurrying forward. "I am so sorry to interrupt your games lesson, Mr Andrews, but could we borrow some children for a photo?"

"As long as they don't break the camera."

Donna groaned inwardly as Mr Andrews laughed at his own joke as he always did and then surveyed the forest of hands and attentive faces. "Donna, Sam, you always put a lot of effort into games, you can go and Matthew, Sami and..." he paused, surveying the faces again.

"That's my dad!" exclaimed Laura petulantly, "Can't I go?"

"Very well, but this is not an excuse for everyone else to stop playing. Let's get back to the game."

Donna followed with the others as Mrs Jarvis bounded across the grass to where Paul Glade was standing with a reporter and photographer. "Hi Dad!" Laura went over to him.

"I'm working, please don't disturb me." Donna watched as Laura's face turned red with embarrassment and she shrank back into the group of children. The photographer stepped forward,

"Right I want a photo of you children, with the Head and Mr Glade standing by the proposed new cycle track and in the background we can see just where the site of Wastecom will be." Donna stood at the back of the group who now clustered around Paul Glade. He was holding a large piece of paper in his hand. "Now Mr Glade, if you wave the plan and then everyone can cheer and you children can show how pleased you will be with your new playground and cycle track."

"The children don't know anything about this, yet," Mrs Jarvis interrupted and Donna noticed a red mark creeping over her crinkly neck. "It was all planned for the newsletter this week."

"That's ok, it won't be going out till next week's edition. Now let me get the children's names," and he rummaged in his bag for a battered notebook. "Now who have we here?"

Donna stood quietly waiting her turn as all the other children pushed forwards except Laura, who was watching her father. Paul Glade was in a world of his own, muttering excitedly to the reporter about the plans. "Yes the entrance to Wastecom will be at the top of the slope, all this scrub land will be cleared for the site and where we are standing will be a cycle track leading from the estate. Over at the back of the school will be the new playground thanks to the generosity of Wastecom, who are buying up all this land. Finally, we will be doing something with this eyesore," he waved towards the scrub land at the edge of the field, "it's just a mess." Donna was brought back to earth by Sam punching her arm as the reporter waited for her name.

"Thank you children, now back to your lessons." Mrs Jarvis dismissed them and turned her attention once again to the reporter and photographer.

"Isn't that where you found your bracelet?" Donna spoke quietly to Sam as they made their way back to the games lesson.

Sam nodded vigorously, "And that's where we build our dens. That's our playing area. They can't have that."

'But that's just what will happen,' thought Donna to herself, unless someone did something to stop them.

The clock hands ticked slowly towards 3.15 and the end of another day. A hush hung over the class as Mrs Jones completed the page she was reading out loud and closed the book. "Your homework over the next two weeks is linked with our project on conservation. I want you all to research a conservation project that has made a difference and you can get started this weekend. Now has anyone any ideas?" There was silence. Donna bent her head over her desk. "Come on Donna, I know your mother has been involved in lots of campaigns!" Mrs Jones stood over her desk as Donna looked around her, hoping someone else had their hand up. Laura was smirking at the back of the class and stuck out her tongue. "Well we won't be going until someone has an idea," Mrs Jones continued.

"Go on, Donna, think of something or we'll be here all day," Sam whispered.

Donna looked around, hoping someone else would have an idea but everyone was staring at her expectantly. "Well," she hesitated, "there's lots about the rainforest, pollution and endangered species. My mum says 'Save the whale' was one of the best and next was stopping the use of CFCs in fridges and aerosols."

Mrs Jones turned her attention back to the class. "Now you have some ideas to start to investigate. Thank you, Donna. You may give yourself a team point."

Donna stood up reluctantly and went over to the chart and carefully coloured in one blue square next to her name. As she went back to her seat, she noticed Laura nudging Shelley and pointing at her. The look on Laura's face was one Donna knew from last term. She would need a quick getaway that evening and so took off her glasses in preparation and put them into her case.

A bell rang shrilly. "Class dismissed. Chairs up and off you go." But just as Donna stood up, Mrs

Jones called her back. "Donna, one moment please." Donna hung back as the class surged past and into the long corridor. "I wonder if you could ask your mother if she could send in any leaflets of information. I know she is very involved in these causes."

"I'll ask her, Mrs Jones." A quick escape was now out of the question. Donna could either hang around in the classroom and risk Mrs Jones' questions or hope that Laura had already gone. Anything was better than facing Laura. She went over to her drawer and pretended to fiddle around, taking things out and putting them back as if she was searching for something.

"Is anything the matter?" Mrs Jones looked up from the pile of books she had just started marking.

"I think I might have left my spare glasses here." Donna hoped she sounded convincing. She rummaged a bit more then looked up. Out of the corner of her eye she spotted Laura just crossing the playground. She was safe. She bent down again and closed her drawer, "No, not here. Must be at home. See you on Monday, Mrs Jones." Donna closed the door and walked slowly up the corridor to put even more time between her and Laura. She picked up her bag which had mysteriously landed on the floor and had footprints on it and looked around for Sam, but he was nowhere to be seen. Slowly she made her way across the playground and over the field, keeping a watch for Laura or for Sam. But the field was deserted.

3.40pm the same day

As Donna opened her front door, she knew that her mother was on yet another cause. The battered leather sandals and multi coloured bag had gone. They were usually dumped in the corner where the remains of the Mother's Day present languished in a brown, shrivelled heap of twigs and dead leaves. A placard leaned against the wall with 'Save the hosp...' dripping its black lettering onto the carpet, missing the open tin of paint. Donna picked up the tin and replaced the lid before noticing the red light of the answer machine. Her mother's breathless voice echoed in the empty house "Sorry precious, emergency meeting. I'll be home at about seven – dinner is in the fridge. Love you."

The familiar sight of a half-finished pile of ironing spilling out of the washing basket, the dishes from breakfast mouldering on the empty dishwasher and a half-eaten cheese sandwich sitting on the kitchen table greeted her. The tickle of soft fur on her legs meant Romeo wanted her attention. She picked up the cat and nestled her face in his black and white warmth. "I don't suppose anyone has fed you." Romeo just purred his agreement as Donna poured clean water and some fresh food into two bowls by the cat flap. The speed with which he started to wolf down his food made Donna feel hungry but it was the thought of eating alone that made her grab some coins and her phone from the dresser and escape through the back door, over the garden fence and down the alley towards the adventure playground where she was certain she would find Sam. At least then she would have some company.

Four small boys on bikes were racing round the swings and climbing frames but they slowed when they saw Donna. "What do you want? This is our den." The biggest brought his bike to a standstill, his front wheel brushing against her feet but she didn't flinch.

"Where's Sam? He's usually here." Donna stared straight at him and pushed the bike wheel away from her.

"Sam who?"

"Sam Maloney… big boy, hair always sticking out," she continued as he frowned.

"Dunno."

Donna turned to go. "He hasn't come out of school yet," the smallest ferrety looking child added as he skidded to a halt.

"How do you know?"

"He lives by me."

Donna looked from one to the other, trying to work out if they were telling the truth and then an idea came to her. Sam must be treasure hunting where he found the bracelet.

"Is he in trouble?" The ferrety child followed Donna as she turned and made her way to the sloping path through the trees that led to the school field. "What's he done?" He speeded up and pulled in front of Donna.

"His mum wants him," Donna lied, hoping he would believe her.

"Oh. See ya." He manoeuvred his bike over the grass verge and back to where his friends were waiting.

Donna jogged down the path, looking here and there for a flash of red amongst the trees and undergrowth. She reached the bridge that ran over the river, pushed her way through the broken down wire fence and walked along the bank, glancing behind her every few steps in case anyone else was around. The land by the river was private property although no one ever seemed to do anything with it and it was covered in litter.

"Sam, are you there?" Donna called out gently. The only answer was the rippling of the water and the mournful twittering of a few late summer birds. Sam was nowhere in sight. Without a thought, she plunged further into the undergrowth. Donna stood still and listened. Apart from the hum of the traffic on the distant ring road there was an eerie quiet. She stepped forward, a twig cracked under her feet and she jumped. "Stupid," she muttered to herself, "Afraid of your own feet are you?" She edged her way forwards, looking from side to side.

"Get in here, quick!" A figure in a red sweatshirt jumped out and grabbed her by the arm, pulling her towards the shelter of a den like structure of brambles where she fell on her knees in the damp leaf mould. Sam crouched in front of her, his finger to his lips. "Don't make a sound. We might be heard."

"Who by, you idiot?" Donna stared at Sam crossly. "What on earth are you doing here, hiding like this?"

For an answer, Sam pulled her further into the woodland and up a slight slope. At the top, the woodland met an old deserted pathway where the railway used to be. A fence now surrounded the waste land at the very top of the slope. A wooden sign had been put up on which had been tacked a pink piece of paper. "Read it" Sam insisted.

"Planning consent for three office buildings, incinerator, storage sheds, a car park and entrance. That's what Laura's dad was going on about this afternoon. A stupid business is going to put up a few offices. Big deal"

"But they can't. Not here," Sam insisted, pointing to a sketch map which clearly showed that some of the building would be on the waste ground on which they were standing.

"Look Sam, there's plenty of other places to

play. It's just a crummy bit of useless land." Sam said nothing. He just pulled Donna back down the slope to his hiding place. Kneeling down, he hastily dug away the damp earth to reveal the shimmering colours of a mosaic of a young girl's face. She was dressed in white and on her arm it looked as if there had been a golden coloured bangle.

"This is where I found the bracelet. This is Annie and this is Annie's home. They can't build here!"

Evening; 161 AD

Marcus leaned back on the couch and held out a clay beaker for the servant to refill it. "Fool, be careful," he spat out, "this is real wine from Rome not the vinegar from this cold place." He leaned back on the couch, pulled his cloak tightly round him and shuddered.

"But what about the child, Marcus?" Livia, his wife spoke gently.

"My wastrel of a brother sends me a slave that he no longer has a use for, gives her freedom and expects me to pay for her upkeep." One hand tugged at the lock of hair on his forehead. "It's always the same. I clear up his mess and make everything right!"

"Shh, the servants will hear." Livia got up from her couch and went over and sat by him. "But now the baby is here, we must do something. Her mother was an excellent servant. I just wonder if we could educate her with Luca. She would be ideal to run the house and perhaps keep me company when you are away …" her voice trailed off.

"Educate them!" Marcus exploded. "What next? They will all demand their freedom if we are not careful."

"Perhaps that would not be a bad thing," Livia murmured.

A log crackled in the grate and the smouldering oil lamps cast a dim light over the room. "I admit it is not the usual practice for slave children to be educated with our own but she could be a companion to Luca when she is older. She would be of high status and could even marry and then we would not be reliant upon the riff raff that arrive from Rome's other, less civilised provinces." Livia shuddered and pulled her cloak ever tighter round her shoulders, "Why it is even said in the market place," her voice dropped to a whisper as she leaned closer to Marcus, "that slaves from Gaul have been known to kill their masters as they slept!"

"Yes and they can grow horns and they kick animal bladders full of air round in groups as a way of entertaining each other," Marcus snorted "You must not believe everything you hear."

Footsteps padded softly over the mosaic flooring. Julia, the nurse leaned over and placed a bowl of almonds on the table in front of Marcus, "And the child would need a wet nurse, you can't expect Julia to look after Luca and another child."

"What do you think, Julia? Could you look after more than one child?" Livia smiled gently, "I know the

Dobunni tribe are considered the best to rear a child."

Julia's grey eyes twinkled in the firelight, "True, some of our forebears even nursed the future emperors of Rome. But it would be hard work..." she paused, "although a few extra sestertii would help. I will get Luca for you now."

"I believe you have set your mind on this, Livia." Marcus smiled. "For once I am prepared to agree. It would be a fine thing if we had our own educated and loyal servants like the Imperial family!"

Julia reappeared, her arms holding a wooden cradle which she placed by Livia. The baby's dark lashes fluttered on his cheeks as he stirred in his sleep. "You had better order an extra cradle, Julia, for you now have two little ones." Marcus poured himself another goblet of wine. "Perhaps she could make a useful marriage with one of the local tribal leaders when she is older." He turned to face Julia, "Look after her well. It will be worth fifty denarii for you each Saturnalia."

Julia hurried back to her room above the

kitchen. She picked up the little baby girl and cradled her, "Now you will grow up like a lady, just as your mother had said and that money will buy us our freedom and perhaps some land or a house for us both." She unrolled a cloak and emptied the contents of a reddish brown pottery jar onto the floor. Amongst the bronze and silver coins shone the emerald eyes of a golden snake bangle. "I will keep this safe for you until you are older and can be a proper lady. I will call you Aurea, like your mother." The baby gurgled happily as Julia dangled the snake bracelet in front of her.

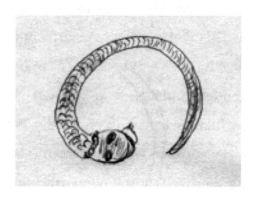

This is the bracelet I found.

Sam

CHAPTER THREE

5.00pm; the present day, Friday 4th September

Sam continued to scrape away at the leaf mould and damp earth. Donna leaned closer. The mosaic was larger than she had expected. All around the central figure were the remains of pictures of animals and the unmistakeable scene of a villa surrounded by fields and trees with a small river running along side. In the background was a large gate like building. "That's the River Churn! It must be," Donna bent down to look closer, "it's just the way it bends."

"That's why they can't build here. This is where she lived. This is Annie's house. It's right here!" He pointed to the scraps of mosaic that made up the villa. " Everyone says Annie has a white dress and so does this girl." He brought out the tissue and unwrapped it to reveal the bracelet, "This is her bracelet!" he held it against the golden coloured tiles. "This is Annie, she lived here and if we search we'll find the villa and everything!" he looked up at Donna expectantly.

"But how, I mean... "Donna struggled to keep up with Sam's thoughts, "...why is this Annie?" she spluttered.

"Easy, " said Sam as he carried on scraping and digging, "ghosts haunt where they live and Annie lived here, which is why she is in the school."

"This isn't the school, though, the school is over there!"

"Well she can walk or float or do whatever ghosts do... this is Annie and this is her house!" Sam sank back on his heels and looked defiantly at Donna.

"So what do you want us to do?"

"Stop them – the buildings and that site up there," he waved his hand towards the top of the slope. "This is Annie's home and it's our play area so it should be left the way it is!" Donna had never known Sam to be so outspoken.

"Well we can't just start digging. We haven't got time and someone will spot us." Donna's heart sank at the enormity of the task ahead.

"I know that! I'm not stupid!" Sam yelled.

"All right, there's no need to get stressy!" Donna flinched.

"I'm sorry Moo cow." Sam paused, "But you're cleverer than me – you'll know what to do."

"I don't know Sam… this is too big… we can't…" her voice faded away.

"Please, we've been friends for years and if you don't know what to do, then no one will. Could we ask your mum?" he added brightly." Your mum would never let anyone destroy something like this. Can't she get a petition or something?" Sam gently began to cover the mosaic.

"I suppose I could say something. But we can't really do this all on our own. We need to tell someone, the museum – anyone, I don't know!"

"Why? You're always saying no one listens to kids," Sam stood up and rubbed the earth from his hands down his trousers. "That's why you won't let me tell Mrs Jones all about Laura and Shelley and what they do."

Donna bit her lip. "That's different."

"No it isn't," Sam insisted. "She threw your bag down on the floor and kicked it around and everyone was laughing today," he paused, "and I saw the note she chucked at you. I know all about what happened last year and I bet you stayed behind today to keep out of her way," Sam added.

Donna's mouth dropped open. "How did you work that out?"

"'Cause that's what I'd do," he paused, and Donna watched as a sly smile came over his face. "If you don't help me, then I will go to see Mrs Jones and I'll tell her everything." He paused, "Just ask your mum what we could do, but don't tell her anything, not just yet. There must be some way we can stop this!"

Donna knew she was beaten. "All right, I'll help you. But I can't promise anything. You know what my mum is like. She gets interested in some things and not others. I'll try to get some ideas and then we can decide what's best to do, but don't tell anyone about Laura or Shelley. It'll only make things worse."

"Ok. But you must talk to your mother today. Come on." Sam turned to go but Donna grabbed his arm.

"No, not right now. She probably isn't home, anyway. Let me do this in my time."

"But you will say something tonight?"

"Yes," Donna hesitated, "or early tomorrow. Meet me at the corner of the road by the crossing tomorrow morning at about nine and I'll tell you what happened but don't be late."

"I won't. Come on 'Moo cow' lets go back to your house and see if your mum's in."

"Sam, there's one more thing."Donna twisted the edges of her sweatshirt and tried not to catch Sam's eye.

"What?"

"Can you please stop calling me Moo cow." Donna blushed remembering the nickname she had somehow acquired after appearing as a cow in the nativity when she was 6 years old.

"But you've always been 'Moo cow' to me." Sam scratched his head and looked puzzled.

"Yeah, but I'd like to be Donna from now on. Just Donna!"

Sam shrugged,"Ok Moo, I mean Donna. Race you to your house," and he ran off up the slope with Donna chasing after him.

Donna was no match for Sam though. "Beat you!" He leaned against the fence, panting.

"You won this time, but I'll win tomorrow!" Donna gasped.

"Just remember your promise to talk to your mum!" he called out as he turned and ran down the alleyway and round the corner to the older part of the estate where he lived. Donna went up the path. Her mother's car was parked in the driveway and there were the sounds of raised voices coming from the lounge. She opened the front door and stood in the hallway, listening.

"What I want to know is why this has all come as a surprise. Surely someone knew what he was up to?" Her mother's voice sounded angry.

"I think the planning notice has been around for ages, but no one thought that this place was big enough for Wastecom. From what I've heard there is a new and very tough Managing Director, Challis I think he's called, who wants to make Wastecom one of the biggest disposal companies in the world. No project is too small and once they've got established in an area, they expand and expand and no one has been able to stop them so far" a quieter male voice replied. Donna leaned further into the doorway.

"Well this may just be the last thing that Paul

Glade does. Wastecom are not going to build here and that is final."

Taking a deep breath, Donna opened the door and stepped into the lounge. Her mother looked up from the floor where she was kneeling surrounded by bits of paper. "Hallo darling. Sorry I wasn't here earlier but there was this meeting about the hospital closures and then I just heard the news." Alison pushed a stray piece of hair from out of her eyes, rolled up the sleeves of the baggy purple sweater which enveloped her and bent again over the newspaper cuttings that were spilling out of a file on the floor.

"What news?" Donna waited as her mother rummaged through the cuttings again.

"About Wastecom. Tom and I, oh this is Tom by the way," a tall thin man smiled at Donna and nodded a 'hello' which Donna ignored. "What was I saying? Oh yes, Tom and I are getting a campaign together." She held up a scrap of paper triumphantly, "Got it, this is what I was telling you about!" She thrust the piece of paper under Tom's nose, and then turned her attention back to Donna. "There's some fish and chips on the table. Tom bought them. Can you heat them up and then bring some through for us? We'll be in the office, and there's some tea in the pot."

Donna went into the kitchen and distributed the fish and chips between three plates and stacked them in the microwave to heat up, then took two into the office where her mother's fingers were now hitting the computer keys as hard as if they had been Paul Glade's face. Tom smiled his thanks and Donna went back and sat down at the kitchen table. Romeo took the opportunity to climb up on her lap and mew piteously. "Looks like it's you and me again, Ro."

She fed him some of the warm battered fish which was exactly what Romeo had anticipated. Donna smiled to herself. At least Sam would be pleased if her mother could stop the plans but why all the fuss about a stupid factory?

10.00pm the same day

It was past ten when the front door slammed and Tom left. Donna was watching a film, curled up on the sofa with Romeo snuggled up next to her. Alison swept into the room and plonked herself down next to Donna, knocking Romeo onto the floor. "Sorry, Romeo but we have important things to discuss." Then she noticed the time, "And you should have been in bed ages ago. It's school tomorrow."

"It's Saturday," Donna explained patiently, picking up the protesting Romeo.

"Oh yes, so it is! Now Tom and I need your help. We know that Paul Glade is going to a big reception at the town hall and about twenty of us are going to wait outside and protest and I want you to come along to show that young people are just as involved in these things as us adults."

Donna sat quietly, "I was going to meet Sam tomorrow morning."

"Oh, this isn't until late afternoon. Then we can have a pizza together in town, what about that? Tom knows a really good place that has just opened," Alison continued eagerly.

"Can't we go together? Just us?" But Donna knew the answer already.

"Another time, next week – will that do?"

Donna nodded, knowing that there would be something important again next week, too. "But why is it so important to stop this company? They can't be that bad."

"Yes they can!" Alison spoke quietly but her eyes blazed. "This company has the worst record as a major exploiter. They say they take our waste and recycle it but all they do is ship it to some poor country over the other side of the world and get them to work for peanuts. And if they do build this incinerator here and these sorting sheds, you can bet the air quality round here will be worse than if we had a twelve lane motorway going through the town."

There was a pause. Donna smiled to herself. This was exactly what Sam had wanted and she hadn't even mentioned the mosaic. This was the perfect time to get the information she needed. "So what sort of things could stop this plan?" she tried to sound as casual as she could, but her heart was beating so loud, she was certain her mother would hear and suspect something.

"Public opinion – no one wants to live near a possible danger to health, but that takes time to get the information and make sure it's accurate."

"What about if there were Roman remains, there?" Donna's heart thumped even more loudly and she felt her hands get sweaty.

"Yes – it's a possibility, but Wastecom could easily build on the top and so nothing would be disturbed – that's what happened at the forum, remember? Time is what we need to delay Wastecom, get the public involved and call for an investigation into their plans. That's why I need you!" and she put her arm around Donna's shoulder. "Then we can make enough fuss, bring this to everyone's attention and stop the plan from going ahead!"

"Ok," Donna spoke reluctantly, "I'll help this time, but please can we go somewhere next weekend?" she added hopefully.

"Of course. I promise." They sat there for a few seconds in peace.

"Now we'd both better get to bed. It's a long day tomorrow, and you," she nodded towards Romeo, "are going outside, like a proper cat."

Alison stood up and brushed a few imaginary cat hairs from her jumper and went out to the kitchen as Donna took Romeo to the front door. Sensing what was about to happen, he shot up the stairs and hid. Donna sighed and closed the door. She went upstairs and into her own room where there was a Romeo shaped lump under the top cover. She slid down, trying not to disturb him. Hopefully her mother's plans to delay Wastecom would satisfy Sam and give her enough time to convince him of the need to show someone what he had found. The last thing she wanted was for him to get stressy and tell Mrs Jones about Laura. With that thought running through her head, she drifted off into an uneasy sleep.

Late afternoon, AD173

Aurea was late. She had promised to help Julia with her spinning from first light but Luca had wanted her help with his studies. It was much later that afternoon when she returned to Julia's work place. "So you remembered, then?" the old woman smiled, "and where is Master Luca?" she continued as Aurea flopped down onto the small couch and picked up her spindle and a handful of the freshly carded wool.

"He is with Marcus, hunting somewhere. They went to catch a wild boar. Luca says he's going to keep it as a pet," Aurea added proudly.

"Another? He has too many animals already," Julia spoke firmly.

"Luca thinks we can tame all wild things and use them for farming!"

Julia sniffed her disapproval. "He should be more mindful of his lessons. Farming won't help a soldier."

"But he's not going to be a soldier. He wants to be a farmer."

"His grandfather was a soldier; his father was a soldier and a fine one too. Luca is expected to follow."

"But Luca would never do what he doesn't want to do!" Aurea insisted but her fingers trembled as she picked up another pile of soft fleece.

"Master Luca will do as he is told!"

There was silence as each was deep in thought. Finally Aurea spoke. "Tell me more about my mother."

Julia sighed, "But you already know everything."

"Then tell me once more, just one more time," Aurea insisted.

"Very well. But keep those fingers moving. I expect all this wool to be completed before we go to bed." Aurea leaned back on the couch and listened intently once more to the story of how her mother had come to England to be the companion of Livia.

"And was my father really an important Senator?" Aurea paused in her work.

"Yes, my girl, your father was the adopted brother of Marcus, our master. It was thought one day he might become Emperor and Marcus would lead the army. But it never happened and so he was sent to Britannia and here he has stayed. Now, get those fingers moving again." Aurea stroked the fleece between the spikes on the carders and teased the threads into a roll before handing them to Julia whose fingers quickly spun them into a fine thread. "Your mother was sent here as a companion to the lady Livia. She had her own furs, jewels and enough money for you and herself. The bracelet you are wearing was a gift from your father. Marcus was often away for months at a time and so they would spend most of the day together. You were born three months after Luca. When your mother died giving birth to you, Livia took on the task of bringing you up and when you marry, you can have the rest of the jewels that your mother brought with her. They are hidden safely."

There was silence again as Julia continued with her spinning. As Aurea picked up the fleece again so the eyes of the snake bracelet sparkled. The sun had finally set when Aurea, her fingers aching with fatigue heard Julia sigh as she put down the spindle. "Now, enough of this. Time for us all to rest before dinner." Julia put away her spindle and took the remains of the wool from Aurea, "And no more talk of the past."

"Thank you, Julia." Aurea kissed the top of her grey head and then went to her room at the far end of the house.

All was quiet and as Aurea curled up on the bed, she stretched out her arm to look at the snake bracelet. The emerald eyes glittered in the moonlight.

This is the place where we make our dens and where I found the mosaic.

Sam

CHAPTER FOUR

9.00am; the present day, Saturday 5th September

Sam was on time for once. He was perched on his bike by the side of the adventure playground, a piece of toast in one hand. He grinned from ear to ear when he saw Donna, "What did she say?"

"Mum knows all about Wastecom and she wants to stop it and she's gong to demonstrate today outside the Town Hall. I'm going along to help. She thinks she can slow everything down. But we can't keep this thing a secret Sam, not for ever." But Donna was talking to herself as Sam had sprung back onto his bike and was already racing towards the steep pathway that led down to the school field.

"Wait for me!" Donna followed as fast as she could as Sam hurtled down the slope. At the bottom, he jumped off and slung his bike into some nettles before diving off the path and into the wasteland that grew along the river bank.

"Not so fast!" Donna picked her way carefully, trying to avoid the brambles. By the time she reached him, Sam was already digging into the earth to reveal the mosaic that he had shown Donna before.

"Come and help, it goes on for ever!"

Donna bent down and scraped away more of the wet earth. For a few minutes they worked in silence until the mosaic spread out in all directions. Finally Donna sat back, rubbed her dirty hands on her jeans and watched for a few minutes as Sam continued scrabbling away, revealing yet more pictures of animals and plants.

"What on earth do you think we can do against a big organisation like Wastecom? We won't be able to stop them for ever. They'll soon find out about all of this. Even my mum reckons big organisations win all the time," a note of despair crept into Donna's voice.

"But if we get in their way enough, they'll go away – just like on the films," Sam continued, smoothing away the earth from the girl's face, stroking it like a pet dog.

"This isn't a film. This is now." Donna paused, "I know it's hard but we ought to tell someone. A big business will have the money to lift this up, take it to a museum and look after it."

"No, never! This was her house. It should be left here, where she lived. We don't want to upset her ghost!" Sam's face flushed angrily.

"There's no such thing as ghosts, Sam!"

"There might be!"

"Mum says it will take ages to get anything done."

"So that means we must do something ourselves. Just promise me you won't say anything!" Donna bit her lip. Sam had never been so animated before. "We can do something. I know we can," he continued.

"Well tonight mum and me are meeting some of her friends outside the town hall. She's organised a protest."

"See, that's a start!" Sam started to cover up the mosaic. "But we need to think of something too." A rumbling sound broke through the still autumn air. Sam looked around quickly and then disappeared into the undergrowth "Keep down and follow me."

Sam led the way up the hillside towards the source of the noise. At the top of the wooded slope, a large metal fence had been put in place. Crouching low, Sam and Donna peeked over the edge. Behind the fence was a bulldozer with a smaller digger. They were both clearing space and a large portable office was being lowered into place by a crane perched on a lorry emblazoned with the word 'Glade Contractors' and in smaller letters underneath, 'For all reasons and in all seasons.'

Sam nudged Donna and pointed to Paul Glade who was busy directing operations. "So that's why he wants the factory here!" Donna whispered.

"We've got to act fast" Sam explained, " It won't be long before the whole area is closed off and if any kids are spotted hanging around, they'll be in trouble!" They both scrambled back down the slope and sat by the stream, listening to the work going on above their heads.

"Soon this whole area will be a mess and then this place won't be ours or hers anymore! We must stop them for ever so that it will always be Annie's special place." Donna noticed the desperation in Sam's voice, but she said nothing. "You said you would help me…" he added slyly, "and remember, I can always tell Mrs Jones about Laura and Shelley."

Donna remained silent. The stream chattered on its way. Above them, the deep grumbling of the bulldozer continued scraping and tearing at the earth. Donna felt the silence stretching ahead and knew she must do something. "Well?" Sam was not going to give up. Donna picked up a twig and slowly and deliberately snapped off a small piece and then another until there was only a stub left. She threw it away.

"All right, you win, but don't expect miracles!" Donna knew when she was beaten. She turned to face Sam, an idea beginning to form in her mind-an idea that might just work.

Sam jumped up, grinning all over his face, "First you must help me to cover the mosaic up, so that no one will know it's here."

Donna nodded, "OK, but let me take a picture first."

"Why?"

"I don't know, but it might just come in useful." She crouched down and got out her phone, twisting and turning it to get the best view.

"Let's see," Sam leaned over to peer at the small images of the girl's face and another of the villa in the background. Then they replaced the earth, spreading it as smoothly as they could and added some large fern leaves over the top. With an extra few dead branches in place, it looked as if some animal had been disturbing the soil, but no one would suspect that anything lay beneath. Donna looked at her watch; it was still only ten o'clock. "How about doing a bit of research?"

"Like reading and writing?" Sam screwed up his face in disgust. Donna giggled. Sam hated school.

"Well we could go to the museum and try to find out if there was ever a house or something here?" Sam looked mutinous. "I've got enough money for chips!" she added.

"And a pickled onion?" Sam always cheered up at the thought of food.

"Yes, I suppose so, but don't you dare breathe pickle over me!"

"Wait on the path. I'll hide my bike." Sam heaved his bike out of the nettles and pushed it further into the bushes. Donna wandered down to the path and waited. The sounds of the building site were punctuated now and then by the unmistakeable sound of Paul Glade calling out instructions. Her mum had said they needed time. Perhaps what she now had in mind would delay things – just for a bit.

"Can we get the chips first?" Sam bounded towards Donna like a large Labrador puppy.

"Idiot, it's only gone ten o' clock. The chip shop doesn't open till eleven!"

Sam's face fell. Donna relented. "Ok, when we get into town, we'll stop at the cake shop."

10.15am; the same day

Ten minutes later, Donna and Sam, his face covered with sugar from a very large donut were peering in through the glass entrance door of the museum. The marketplace was crowded with shoppers but the museum was eerily quiet.

"What now?" Sam brushed sugar from his mouth and licked the last grains from his dirty fingers. Donna shuddered.

"Don't you ever think about germs?"

Sam shook his head. "Well, what do we do now?"

"Shhh. I'm thinking," Donna pushed open the door and looked around.

"You can go in, you know. It's free for children." Donna turned and looked into a pair of piercing green eyes. "Don't look so scared, you're welcome to visit without your parents." The woman smiled, her long red hair falling in a cascade around her face. "Now if you'll excuse me, I need to start work." She pushed past Donna and Sam.

"You mean you work here? In the museum?" Donna asked, an idea beginning to form in her brain.

"Yes, actually, I manage the collections of objects," a slight hint of pride crept into her voice.

"Wow, then could you just answer one question

because you probably know everything about the museum?" Donna's voice must have conveyed exactly the right amount of admiration as the woman continued,

"Well I probably know more about Roman Corinium than most people. How can I help you?" And she stepped through the doors which automatically slid open in front of them. They followed and stood awkwardly in the unusual surroundings of the museum. "Go, on, ask away. I won't bite! I'm Doctor Maisie Vine," and the lady held out a long slim hand covered with silver rings. Donna and Sam shook her hand.

"Are you a real doctor? Like at the hospital?" Sam asked.

"Sorry. I'm just a Doctor of Archaeology, not medicine. But it does mean I can answer most people's questions about Cirencester. Now fire away!"

"Well, what we want to know is if there were ever any buildings or a part of the town on our school field. That's by the River Churn," Donna added as explanation.

"Come with me," picking up her bag, she led the way through the galleries to an artists' reconstruction of the town. The light was low and a soft carpet hushed every footfall. They all stopped by a large glass case in which was a model of the town in Roman times. Dr Vine pointed to the model. "Now over here is the River Churn and the town went as far as this area here which is your school car park."

"Are you sure?" Donna asked desperately.

"I'm afraid so. The Roman people were keen never to build too close to the river as it did flood and the water is described as a rushing torrent that destroyed whole buildings! Of course this model is of Corinium in the 4th century AD. There might have been small villas dotted here and there at an earlier date, but we have no evidence.

Sam leaned over and pressed his nose against the glass, "But there must be something. We've found a mosaic."

"Yes, just some stones," Donna butted in quickly and glared at Sam to shut him up, "which we found in the river."

"That's not unusual. Bits of pottery and mosaic turn up everywhere in this town, but there has always been a story that there was a villa over here," and she pointed to an area by the river close to the school field. "But I am afraid there is no evidence. It's just a story, like the story of Annie, haunting the school!"

"How do you know about her?" Sam interrupted.

"Because I was told that very same story when I was at school and we all know there's no such thing as ghosts! Now, enjoy your visit and bring your family next time. If you need to know anything, there are some more exhibits upstairs and good luck! I hope you find out what you need." Doctor Vine went back through the galleries towards the main entrance.

Both children stared at the model. "Well, what

now?" Sam looked forlornly at Donna.

"Nothing! We have all the information we need!"

"How? That lady said it was just a story, abut the house, I mean."

"Yes but it was exactly the place where Wastecom want to build their factory!" Sam looked puzzled. Donna sighed, "Don't you see, if there is a story going round about a house on the site people are far more likely to want to stop the development. Remember the phrase Mrs Jones taught us, 'there's no smoke without fire'," she added triumphantly. "All we need to do is make sure more people get to hear about this mystery house. That will delay things and it might take ages before anything is found and every day is good news. If it takes long enough, this Wastecom company might just go somewhere else."

"So how can we make sure people find out?"

"Just wait and see!" Donna looked at her watch. "Come on, race you to the chippy!"

12.30pm; the same day

By the time Donna got home, it was past midday. She had left Sam in the wasteland by the river. He was still digging, hoping to find more buried treasure. Donna had made him promise to come and get her if he found anything new. As she opened the front door, she was confronted by a large sign. 'Say No to Wastecom.' Alison was sitting on the floor of the hall, surrounded by bits of paper and half painted placards, her phone clamped to the side of her head. Donna bent down to pick up one of the pieces of paper. It was a newspaper cutting with details of Wastecom and the pollution it had caused in other parts of the world.

"I know – Wastecom are trying to come here to this very town… this is one battle we must win!" her mother's voice called down the phone shrilly, "Right then, make sure you're at the town hall this evening."

"Mum, you look busy, is there anything I can

do to help?" Alison looked up, her eyes sparkling, a sure sign that she was about to embark on another of her schemes and that meant Donna could drop a few hints about the villa.

"But darling, you usually hate anything to do with my work?" Alison frowned.

"Not this time. You see, Sam plays in that area, we all do, make dens, I mean. Well, when Sam was digging by the river bank, he found some mosaic stones, just like the ones in the museum. So there might be real treasure there and some people say there was a villa right where Wastecom want to build!"

Alison scratched her head and left a streak of black paint down one side of her face. "Or people might think that there is treasure…," she paused, "and we can certainly work that into the campaign. 'Stop Wastecom's vandalism of historic sites!' That'll make a good placard for this evening. Now let me show you this."

Thirty minutes later, curled up on the sofa, a

half eaten sandwich on her lap and surrounded by bits of paper, and Alison was explaining why Wastecom would build over her dead body. Donna listened and fed bits of tuna to Romeo who purred his pleasure at yet another meal.

"And they want to site this next to a school!" she exploded.

"But, mum, just what is so bad about Wastecom?"

Grabbing hold of a pile of papers and sorting through them, Alison thrust one under Donna's nose, "Just read this – pollution… rubbish…cases of unexplained illness… they dump everything on to Third World countries to make a profit and help us feel good. And this is just one example. All of these say the same thing!" She threw the papers down in disgust. "What more do you want?"

"But I don't understand, "Donna went on, "How does what we do affect other countries?"

Alison rummaged again through the papers again and pulled out another photocopy which she skimmed through. "Here it is. Wastecom will set up a plant in Cirencester to sort all the recyclable waste in their enormous buildings which will be an eyesore. Some of the stuff they will burn here releasing who knows what into the atmosphere. The rest they will send overseas to be destroyed, usually by burning in some poor place in China or Africa. They'll charge our Council a fortune, but only pay the workers a pittance and the Council will feel good and we'll feel good because we are recycling, but all we are doing is dumping our waste on someone else. It is totally irresponsible."

"So what can we do?"

"Petitions, marches, protests and we start tonight. Then first thing on Monday I am going to see your Head teacher. Surely she won't want this on her doorstep?"

Donna bit her lip, "Don't make too much fuss at school, will you?" remembering her mother's out bursts at a recent PTA event when she realised they did not use Fair Trade coffee.

"Darling I will be charm itself. I need to get the

old bag on side before I can do anything else. Now I must get in contact with… no I'll make a list of all the things I need to do… Can you wash up for me? And check out the local news, there might be something we can use. Remember to be ready for six. Tom is coming to collect us then," and she disappeared into her office.

Donna collected up the plates and went into the kitchen. She filled the sink with lots of hot water and squirted in enough washing up liquid to make masses of frothy, soapy bubbles. Her mother always insisted on using just the tiniest amount of warm water and a dribble of washing up liquid. Donna sighed as she plonked each plate in the water and watched the soap suds fly everywhere. Saving the planet was hard work!

6.00pm; the same day

By the time Tom arrived at six o clock Donna had

changed into clean jeans and a dolphin sweatshirt with dolphin earrings and a pair of bright pink baseball boots. She reached the top of the stairs and waited. Her mother was a flurry of activity, rushing here and there and all the time carrying on a running conversation with whoever would listen.

"Right, banners! Can they go in the boot? No? in the back of the car, then." Donna hung back, leaning on the banister and tried to creep down stairs without her mother seeing her. "There you are, be a good girl and take these leaflets out to Tom," and she dumped a large box into Donna's hands.

Donna went out to the car and scrambled onto the back seat, wedging herself by the side of three large cardboard notices, hastily tacked onto sticks, the box of leaflets on her lap. She squeezed into as small a space as possible, away from the placards which oozed black paint everywhere. Taking out her tissue, she wrapped it round the sticks to keep them both upright and away from her clean jeans.

Tom got into the car, "Sorry about the mess. Here have this cloth."

Donna smiled gratefully, "Thanks," and she spread the cloth over her jeans.

"You look very smart; my sister likes dolphins, too. Have you ever been swimming with them?" He smiled at her in the rear view mirror. Donna was about to reply when her mother arrived,

"Right that's the lot. Off to the Town Hall" and she climbed into the front seat and slammed the car door shut. For a minute Donna thought Tom raised his eyebrows in amusement or exasperation. Perhaps he wasn't so bad after all.

A few late Saturday afternoon shoppers were still wandering up through the market place as Tom drove towards the Town Hall. He parked the car outside Donna's favourite shop. As she climbed out, her gaze turned towards the blue and pink tops and bags on display. "Exploited rubbish" snorted her mother. "Here take these placards and follow Tom."

'At least they're pretty,' thought Donna to herself as she joined the motley crew milling around the entrance to the town hall. 'Why can't they dress fashionably, like normal people?' Donna shuddered and rolled up the sleeves of her sweatshirt to protect it from the damp paint of the placards and waited for more instructions.

But before anyone could say anything, a large sleek black car swept up to the entrance and stopped. The Mayor stepped forward from the doorway and stretching out his hand in welcome opened the car door. Paul Glade got out and hastily straightened his tie.

"Say no to Wastecom! Say no to Wastecom!" Donna's mother started up the chant, which was soon copied by the rest. Before she knew what was happening Donna was thrust at the front of the group, "Join in," her mother hissed "and wave that!" She thrust a banner at Donna. It read, ' Save our heritage. Say No to Wastecom.'

Donna slowly waved it from side to side and

watched as Paul Glade was joined by a very pregnant lady, a teenage boy whom Donna thought was quite cute and then, her heart sank. Climbing out of the back seat was Laura. Donna tried to hide behind the placard but her eyes met Laura's and she noticed Laura's look of surprise. Laura tossed her hair back from her face and followed her father into the Town Hall. The chanting subsided and Donna turned to see her mother, her face flushed in triumph announce to the group, "That went quite well, don't you think?" but Donna knew Laura now had yet another perfect excuse to pick on her even more.

Morning; AD173

"Aurea, come here, I've caught another crayfish." Luca waded deeper into the fast flowing stream and plunged his hands under the stones to bring out a grey, scaly creature which wriggled as it tried to escape the boy's tight grasp. Aurea leaned forward and grabbed a thin arm, steadying him as he scrambled up the muddy bank. "There, in you go." Luca dropped the crayfish into a large round pot where it met three other poor captives.

Aurea's blonde curls tumbled over her shoulders as she peered into the pot,

"How many more do you need? Your father is getting impatient; we should have been at lessons at first light!"

"Only one more! Don't be cross with me, I want to catch one for each of us for this evening. Mother will be so pleased."

"But we can go to the market to buy some!" Aurea sighed, although it was useless trying to reason with Luca. Once his mind was set upon a task, nothing would stop him.

"Wait here with me and we'll go back together," he shouted as he waded back into the stream, his legs red with the cold and his short tunic tucked into his belt.

Aurea sat back on the bank, pulling at the tufts of grass and daisies that grew there.

"Hurry, Luca. I am supposed to come and fetch you; Marcus is here for our lessons."

"Wait, I've nearly… got you!" Luca plunged his hands into the stream and grabbed another crayfish by its tail. "Now we can go back," he announced triumphantly as he dropped the squirming creature into the pot, where it joined its brothers and sisters.

Holding the pot as if it were full of gold, Luca clambered out of the stream and up the bank to where Aurea was waiting. "Come on then," and he turned to go back to the villa. Aurea stood up, brushing away the strands of grass that had fallen in her lap. The sun shone warm on her back, the stream gurgled and splashed its way over the stones and birds twittered in the trees. The sunlight shone through the spring leaves and cast a dappled light over the grassy bank. She had a home, a best friend in Luca and was learning how to read and write. She was far luckier than many other slave children without a mother or father, she thought as her hand touched the gold snake bracelet which she always wore.

Midday; the same day AD173

"But Marcus, how can these marks mean anything?"Luca stared at the shapes scratched in the dust and prodded at them with his toe.

"See here, is an L which starts your name..." the old man explained again to the frustrated Luca. "Just practice the shape one more time on the wax. When it is perfect, you may use a pen and ink like Aurea." Luca picked up the stylus again but suddenly Livia descended on the children.

"Do come and see the new mosaic. I need your help."

"Does that mean lessons are over?" Luca jumped up and looked up hopefully into her face.

"Of course not, but come and see this, both of

you," and she beckoned to Aurea to follow. She led the way to the triclinium. The couches had been removed, the walls had been newly painted with brightly coloured patterns and shapes on a yellow background and there, squatting on the floor, surrounded by thousands of pieces of stone was Trimalchio. His hands moved swiftly over the floor, picking a stone, tapping it into place or calling to his team to smooth another area or to fill in the gaps with fine white sand. Once he had put in place the outlines of the scenes, the main parts were completed by others. He kept the most difficult and detailed parts for his skill alone.

The mosaic stretched over the whole floor of the room. The central part showed a villa, with a small stream and the new entry gate to Corinium in the background. Around this were pictures of all the wild animals, birds and flowers that could be found in the woods and fields around the villa. "It's our home!" Aurea looked up at Livia who smiled proudly.

"That's quite right and that is why I want you

two," she nodded towards Luca and Aurea. At the entrance to the room were the beginnings of two almost life size figures. "I want Trimalchio to model your faces for these two figures. Let him see you, child," she turned Aurea's face with her hand, "and he can add your bracelet on this arm here," she pointed with a slim foot to the figure stretching out a hand towards the other. I want this mosaic to show you children playing here against the backdrop of our villa. This will be far better than our neighbours who want hunting dogs in the centre!" she shuddered.

The workman's hands flicked over the stones and Aurea gasped. Was this really her and was this Luca? The outline shape of her face started to appear in the sandy floor. Trimulchio nodded towards Livia. "Now back to your studies. I am paying Marcus good money to teach you reading, writing and how to count. The floor will not be finished for many days and you will be called again if needed."

"But why do we have to learn such boring

things?" Luca's face turned pleadingly to his mother.

"Aurea doesn't find her studies boring, do you? You must follow her example and grow wise like your father. Now back to work. Trimalchio can come and collect you when he needs to check on the mosaic." With that she turned on her heels and went inside the inner courtyard to prepare for her usual visit to the bath house.

Saturday 5th September; evening

Donna stood quietly as Laura and her family disappeared inside the Town Hall. "Thanks everyone, mission accomplished. Let's all go home for a well deserved rest and plan the next onslaught." Donna watched as her mother, her face flushed and her eyes shining collected up the banners and jammed them in the back of the car. "Come on, darling, Tom's taking us for pizza."

"But aren't we going to wait? I mean is that all there is?" Donna hurried after her mother and tugged at her arm, "I thought we were here all night!"

"We've made our point and Paul Glade knows we're onto him. There's no point waiting here until he's finished stuffing his face on freebies!" Alison climbed into the front seat of the car and Donna squeezed herself onto the back seat. Donna noticed her mother peering at her in the rear view mirror. She suddenly turned round and patted Donna's arm, "Darling I really think you're upset! But don't worry; we've got lots more to do! We've only just begun and Tom's coming round tomorrow so we can plan the next part of this campaign!" She turned to Tom, "Now where's this Italian restaurant, Tom. I'm starving!" Tom switched on the engine.

Donna leaned back and frowned, 'This won't get the quick fix that Sam wanted,' she thought to herself. But what else could they do?

"Not over twenty miles per hour in an urban area for fuel economy remember," Alison prattled on as Tom drove off. Donna caught his eye in the mirror and this time, he definitely did raise his eyebrows. He wasn't that bad after all!

The same evening; 9.00pm

"Well that was a fantastic evening. The Mayor was very complementary about my links with Wastecom and even suggested that I run for Mayor when he retires! I know it must have been very boring for you two," he turned to Laura and Jamie, "but it is important that we are a united family. Now, there's a little surprise for you in my office, Laura and Jamie, we'll talk about driving lessons first thing in the morning."

Laura didn't wait to hear Jamie's reply. She rushed into the office and there on the desk was a box, wrapped beautifully in silver and pink paper with pink ribbons. Inside was the phone she had been telling Shelley about. She turned, to see her father leaning against the doorway. "Sarah wrapped it for me. So your old dad's not so bad after all, is he?"

"You're brilliant!" she flung herself at him and gave him a big hug. "It's just what I wanted!"

" Remember to thank Sarah as well," he added.

"I'll do it tomorrow! Promise!" and Laura rushed up to her room. If she took a photo of her new phone with her old phone, she could send it to Shelley. Just wait till she told everyone else about this at school on Monday!

The river Churn as it flows through the school field, near the place where Sam found the mosaic.
Donna

CHAPTER FIVE

Monday 7th September 9.30

A hush went over the classroom. Laura bit her lip and handed the phone to Mrs Jones. She tossed her hair and stood waiting for the icy, cutting words that were her trademark. "You have been told on numerous occasions about your phones." As she spoke she emphasised the plurals. "Do you think I am stupid? Or that I forget what I have told you already?" She stood still and silent waiting for a reply. Laura said nothing, her face set like stone. "Well?"

The whole class held their breath. Sam nudged Donna who bent her head lower over her book. The slightest move could have Mrs Jones turn her anger on them. "You have deliberately disobeyed me. Again! I will be contacting your father tonight."

The word 'father ' acted like a spark on a dry bed of straw. Laura tried to think of a way to wriggle out of this. It was because of her father that she had the phone with her. The row on Sunday had been spectacular even for Laura. Just because she had forgotten to say thank you to Sarah. Then it just got worse and worse until her father had threatened to take the phone away. That's why Laura had hidden it in her school bag.

"It's only a phone. I just forgot it was in my bag," mumbled Laura, hoping that Mrs Jones would think it was all a mistake. Donna's heart sank when she heard those words. Didn't Laura realise that the best thing to do when Mrs Jones was in a rant was to say nothing, admit to everything and then apologise?

"It is yet another time when I cannot trust you," Mrs Jones continued. "I am tired of this deliberate defiance."

"I said I am sorry," Laura's voice faltered slightly.

"Sorry is not good enough. Now sit down and let me get on with the job I am paid to do which is to teach you." The filing cabinet clattered shut, "Furthermore I am not happy with the way you speak to me."

"I said I'm sorry. It's only a stupid phone!" Laura shrugged her shoulders, an edge of defiance creeping into her voice There was a deathly hush in the classroom.

"I have had enough of this rudeness and answering back."

"What? I said I'm sorry!"

"That's enough!" Mrs Jones sat down at her desk and opened her plans for the day. "Take your books and go to the office. I refuse to teach someone who answers me back like that. Donna, take Laura to the office. I want you to make sure that she gets there. She will work on her own until I am happy to have her back in my class."

Donna stood up reluctantly. This was yet another excuse Laura would have to begin her bullying again. "Quickly, I have not got all day and neither have you!" Mrs Jones snapped. Laura gathered up her books and flounced over to the door. Donna held it open for her and then closed it as quietly as she could. In silence they walked up the corridor. Donna expected a few nasty remarks, but when she took a peek at Laura, she noticed her eyes were glistening. Half way up the coridoor, Laura stopped and turned to face Donna.

"Does your mum still want to stop Wastecom?"

"How did you know?"

"Saw her emails to my dad," she looked at Donna from underneath her curls, "and I saw you on Saturday, at the Town Hall. I had to go there and pretend to be part of this one big happy family. The Mayor wanted to know about Wastecom and dad pretended it was all his idea and said what a great thing it was for the town!"

Donna said nothing and they went a few more steps in silence.

"I can help, you know," Laura spoke in a whisper.

"Why would you want to help me or my mum?" Donna whispered back, thinking of all the times Laura and Shelley had made her life a misery.

"I couldn't care less about your mum or you. This way I can get my own back on dad – it will serve him right if the whole Wastecom thing is stopped."

"Why do you want to do that?"

"It will serve him right! You know I said we had to pretend to be one big happy family – well we're not. Nothing's been the same since, well you know..." Laura's voice tailed away.

Donna nodded, remembering the time in year four when Mrs Jarvis had come into the class and explained about Laura's mother, how ill she was and how everyone had to be kind to Laura.

"But then dad had to bring her into the house and everything changed." She emphasised the word 'her'.

Donna must have looked confused because Laura continued, "Sarah – my dad's girlfriend."

"What do you think you could do?" Donna spoke slowly, not really believing that anything would happen. Part of her wanted to listen to Laura, but part of her wanted nothing to do with whatever Laura had planned.

"I know where his keys are so I can get into the office. Then you can find out exactly what he is doing and where he's going! Your mum and her creeps and geeks can embarrass him even more by turning up everywhere he goes. He's really terrified of upsetting this man who's in charge of Wastecom."

Donna felt her face go pink at the description of her mother's friends even though she knew it was at least partly true. She thought for a moment, but it might be her only chance of stopping

Wastecom. There was silence as they continued up the corridor.

"Well?" Laura stopped outside the office.

"There's Sam… he wants to help too. I can't leave him out," Donna explained.

"Your boyfriend can come along if you like. Meet me after school on the field by the stream." Laura barged into the office and Donna made her way back to class with a lot of decisions to make and quickly. She slid into the seat next to Sam.

'OK?' he mouthed at her. She nodded, "Laura is on our side!"

"What?" he said out loud then realised his mistake and turned it into a cough.

"Is there someone else who would like to join Laura in the office?" Mrs Jones looked up from her marking.

"Sorry Mrs Jones," Sam added and bent his head over his books. "But can you trust her?" he whispered.

"I have to – if we want to do something fast, she's our only hope!"

Morning; AD 171

Aurea took the stylus and quickly corrected Luca's letters. She pressed her fingers to her lips and handed it back. "Marcus, Luca has finished his work. May we go now?" Her words startled the old man who had taken the chance to close his eyes in the warm sunshine. Aurea held out the wax tablet. "Look, all correct."

"And how much help did you have, Master Luca?"

"I did most of it," he mumbled.

"But not enough!" Marcus paused but his frown turned to a smile. "I will tell your mother you have both done well today. There will be time in the winter for study. It is a beautiful day and the market will be busy. Go and enjoy yourselves."

Aurea grabbed Luca by the hand, "Then tell her we will eat in the market," she called. "I have money," and the two of them ran out of the villa grounds and down the path towards the town.

The path gave way to an elaborate mosaic pavement that followed the straight lines of the roads and alleyways that all led to the forum. Crowds of people were making their way towards the amphitheatre where a religious festival was taking place. Sheep, goats and chickens wandered here and there, getting in everyone's way and occasionally trying to steal food from the open fronted shops. Handcarts loaded with fruit and vegetables trundled along the paved roadways. Each shop had its own pungent smell which mixed with the odour of squashed fruit and the droppings left behind by the animals. Aurea bought a small loaf and slices of roast pork and divided it between the two of them.

A crowd had gathered in the forum to listen to a storyteller proclaiming the great deeds of the Roman armies. Aurea and Luca squeezed their way to the front and listened, the juice from the roast pork running down their chins. A tall centurion was standing nearby, listening intently. Luca nudged Aurea, "My father wants me to be a soldier, like him." He threw the remains of the food into the dust and ground it to a pulp under his foot. His voice dropped to a whisper. "He is sending me to Rome."

"When?" Aurea's voice faltered.

"After Saturnalia, when the better weather comes."

"Is that what you want?"

"What do you think? I have no wish to kill or be killed. I always wanted to stay here and learn to farm. This is my home."

"Can't you tell him?" Aurea continued.

"No, it is all decided. I must be away for three years, but when that time is up I can return here."

Aurea threw the half-eaten meat into the gutter where it was seized upon by a mangy dog that sloped off into the shadows. "Will I ever see you again?"

"Of course," Luca looked at her intently. "After three years, I am coming back here. We will make our farm together." He took a small knife from his money bag and pricked the tip of his index finger. A drop of blood oozed out, "Give me your hand. We will make a blood promise." Aurea held out her hand and waited for the stab of pain, but Luca was quick. She felt a sharp jab, then a tiny trickle of red spread over her fingertip.

"Do you promise?" Luca demanded, holding her finger close to his.

"Promise what?"

"Promise that you will wait and I promise that I will return."

Aurea nodded, "I promise!" Luca pressed her finger onto his.

"The blood is sealed on our promise. It can never be broken." Luca jumped to his feet. "Now until I leave, I want to explore the fields and woods, to ride over the hills and swim in the stream," he held out his hand to Aurea, "and you will come with me."

It was only later that Aurea realised that from

that moment on, she no longer felt like a child. Even though they did as Luca had wanted and explored the woods and hillsides it was in the knowledge that it would all soon end.

Monday 7th September 3.30pm

The last few families were crossing the bridge at the far end of the school field when Donna and Sam met Laura. She was leaning on the rickety fence overlooking the stream and kicking at a discarded can. Donna slowed her pace, but Sam bounded ahead. "Donna says you can help us stop this…" he gestured towards the wasteground where clearing would soon start.

"You can find out all my dad's plans and then your mum," she turned to Donna, "can really annoy him." She smiled sweetly, "That will serve him right. You know Jones told my dad all about the phone and he said I wasn't allowed to take it to school. So when I get home I'll be in even more trouble." She kicked at the can again.

Donna stood silently, biting her lip, not knowing what to say. "So what's so important about this scrubby bit of land? It's only nettles and junk," she picked up the can and threw it far into the brambles.

"Shall we tell her, Sam?"

"Tell what? Have you two got a secret?" Laura giggled.

"Come on." Sam bounded off the path and led the way down into the undergrowth and stopped at a patch where the earth was damp and clear of weeds. He carefully scraped the soil away to reveal the mosaic. Laura peered closer.

"So what? The local museum will lift it up and put it somewhere on show."

"No," Sam jumped to his feet. "This is her home and it should stay here." Donna put her hand on his arm and shook her head as a warning.

"Whose home?"

"Annie's."Sam insisted. "This is where she lived, this is her, everyone says that she wears a white dress..." he pointed to the white tiles in the mosaic and I found this." He brought out the snake bracelet and put it alongside the golden tiles by the girl's arm. "Ghosts don't like being disturbed!"

"There's no such thing as ghosts," Laura laughed, then shrugged her shoulders. "Suits me, though – you get to be some kind of hero, you can help your mum," she turned to Donna, "and I can get my own back on darling daddy and his stupid plans." She spat out the final words.

"What do you think we can do?"Donna spoke hesitatingly.

"A few accidents can slow things down." Laura jerked her head towards the top of the slope where Wastecom had already set up a small compound surrounded by metal fencing. A bulldozer could be heard growling and clearing more space for the development. "Come with me."

Sam and Donna covered up the mosaic and

together they climbed up the slope to where they could see into the compound.

"Those things make such a mess and are so dangerous." Laura gestured to he bulldozer. "We could just put it into gear and let it go," she giggled. "My brother did that when dad brought one home to clear the garden. It went straight into the fence and knocked down half the garage. Mum was so mad," she paused and her voice trembled, "that was my real mum, not Sarah, I mean." She paused, "So, if I go home and get the site keys, we can meet back here at 4.30. Then we can have some fun."

"But I thought we were just going to get his diary and..." Donna's voice died away.

"We will, but as I said, a few accidents will really upset everybody!" Laura's eyes sparkled.

Sam frowned and bit his lip, "How will that help?"

Laura took a deep breath and began to explain slowly, "If there's an accident, there will be an enquiry and that will hold things up. That means we get time to think up some more ideas. I'll meet you back here at 4.30." She swung her bag over her shoulder and clambered through the undergrowth towards the road. Sam and Donna went back to where the mosaic was hidden and added more branches to cover it up properly.

Sam suddenly stopped and looked at Donna, "I don't like this."

Donna nodded, "Listen Sam, we'll go along with Laura just this once, but if you're not happy and it doesn't work, then we must tell someone at school or at the museum. They'll know what to do." Sam looked up at Donna, "That's a promise, Sam." He nodded and added some more leaves to the earth as if to disguise the place from prying eyes.

"Just tell your mum you're meeting me at my place and I'll tell my mum I'm meeting you at yours – they'll never bother checking up."

In silence they made their way back onto the path and headed for the main road. At least they now had some sort of plan of action, even if Donna was not certain where things would end.

CHAPTER SIX

Monday 7th September, 4.00pm

As Laura walked up the path, she could hear raised voices from the kitchen. Her father and Sarah were arguing, something which usually would have made her smile with satisfaction. But this time she could hear exactly what they were talking about and it was her, "But she is still a child and it was only a phone, after all!" Sarah pleaded.

"That is not the point, I do not like being disobeyed and this is not the first time," her father paused for breath. "I have made up my mind that unless she changes her attitude towards you and this family and starts to follow our instructions, this is not the place for her. We have the money left from her mother's will which was to be kept for her. It will pay for a boarding school."

Laura stood perfectly still and waited, her hand trembling against the door frame. "We can tell her tonight after supper." Paul Glade continued, "It's been in my mind for some time that things were not working out as I had expected and with the baby on the way it will be best for all of us. In fact I went to see a school last week, not far away, very good reputation and plenty to do after school and at weekends." There was a pause. The screeching sounds of a computer game drifted down from Jamie's open window. Laura waited for Sarah to say something in her defence.

An age passed. Laura held her breath, willing Sarah to speak. When the words eventually came, they were faltering and hesitant but the message was clear. "You're right. Laura is spoilt and it is time someone made her realise that the world does not revolve around her. Goodness knows I've tried my best but she just seems to do things deliberately to annoy and upset me."

Laura had to stuff her fist in her mouth to stop herself from shouting out. How dare they plan all this together! "Then it's agreed," Paul continued. "I will phone up the school now and make an appointment for a visit before the end of this week. The number is in the phone book."

Laura crouched down away from the glass panel in the front door, her heart pounding. There was no time to waste. With Jamie in his bedroom and her father in the hall, she had to get into his office. Crawling along under the windows, she crossed the front lawn and round the side of the house, where she dumped her school bag behind the recycling box. The side gate was open as always and she tried the handle of the old utility room which her father now called his office. It was not locked. She opened the door slowly and peeked inside. On the desk was an open briefcase.

Tiptoeing across the floor, Laura stopped by the desk. Hardly daring to breathe, she pulled the briefcase closer and started to sort through the jumble of papers and files. Somewhere inside, there must be a set of keys,

"So that's settled, tomorrow at 10.00am," her father's voice was getting closer. He must be using his mobile phone and not the landline in the hall. The keys were not in the briefcase. In desperation, Laura pulled open the top drawer. Inside was a bunch of keys with a dirty plastic label attached with the words 'Site office' scrawled in blue biro. Laura grabbed them and fled through the door just as her father entered. There was no time to close it after her and any movement would have made her father suspicious. She stood quite still, clutching the keys so tightly that she felt the metal dig into her hands.

Paul Glade was still engrossed in the phone call, "So that would make the annual fees about £9000, right?" Laura could hear the footsteps getting closer, crossing the floor. He must have noticed the open door. If he saw her and the keys he'd know she was up to something. She desperately tried to think of a reason for being there. The footsteps stopped by the door. Laura held her breath.

"Of course I do understand there will be extra costs for some activities. But we can sort that out at a later date." The door started to close. Her father was only centimetres away. Laura was about to jump out from behind the door, with the keys in her hand and pretend she had found them outside when the door was suddenly pulled shut and the key turned in the lock. Paul Glade's mind was on other things, "So what sort of extra curricular activities are there?" Laura had heard enough. Keeping low, she retraced her footsteps round the side of the house, across the front garden and made her way back to the school field. There were important things to do.

Monday 7th September, 4.10pm

Donna slung her bag on the hall floor. "I'm home." Frantic tapping drew her to her mother's 'office '. "Hi mum!" The figure hunched over the keyboard looked up briefly before resuming her typing.

"Oh, hallo, love. Good day at school?"

"Yeah. Spose," Donna edged closer, intrigued by this intense concentration. "What are you doing?"

"Emailing about that firm Wastecom. They are no more than exploiters, polluters." Crash went the fingers on the keyboard. "They must be stopped but everything takes such a long time and the site's already been set up."

"What do you mean?" Donna perched on the table edge and peered at the screen. There was a pause as her mother looked up, her eyes flashing with exasperation.

"We need time – loads of it to do things

properly and make everyone take notice. What I can't understand is how it all got so far without anyone knowing."

"How could you get more time?"

Alison swivelled round in her chair to face her daughter, "The best way to stop this is to prevent the building work from going ahead, even temporarily. Then we can get the local people against the project. If only someone could discover something on the site or for there to be an accident of some sort. That usually delays things for ages, years even."

Donna smiled to herself. Laura had suggested just the same thing! "I'm going round to Sam's to do some homework. I might even have tea round there. Is that ok?"

"Good idea but make sure you're home before eight," Donna nodded but her mother had already turned her back on her and had resumed her furious typing.

Monday 4th September, 4.30pm

Donna reached the bridge first. The water, deeper than usual after the long wet summer, roared over the stones, a bird whistled in the late afternoon air but the site was quiet. The high fencing around the site hid everything from prying eyes, just as Laura had said. Footsteps clattered down the slope and Donna turned to see Sam, his face flushed from running. "Where's Laura?" he panted

"Dunno" Donna shrugged and turned back to watching the water. "She'll be here. I know it."

"Ready?" Laura ran up to them, dangling some keys from her fingers. "Look what I found? This is all we need to get inside!"

"But how did you get them?" stammered Donna.

"I stole them and daddy dearest won't even know they've gone. He's far too busy trying to get rid of me!" Donna shuddered at the venom in Laura's voice.

"Are you scared?" Laura rattled the keys in front of Donna's eyes. "If you're not in with me, I'll do this all on my own and then you'll be sorry."

"No it's not that, but how do we get in the site? We can't just go up to the gate and open it in full view of the road."

"No need, we just go up to the fence along this slope and lift up one of the fence panels. Do either of you know a way to get to the top?" Laura surveyed the tangled mess of brambles and shrubs.

"I do," Sam said slowly, catching Donna's eye, "there's a short cut. I use it if I'm late for school in the morning. Follow me."

He led the way through the undergrowth by the stream and up a steep path that had been flattened by countless slithering and sliding feet. The trees on either side served as a make shift handrail for when the slope got too slippery. Using these, the three were soon at the top standing along a narrow ledge on which balanced the high metal fence. Sam peered at the gaps between the panels. "It's all quiet."

"Now, when I say 'lift' grab hold of the bottom of this panel and yank it away from the base," Laura commanded. "Ready, lift!" The panel tilted and swayed as it was eased away from the heavy base. "Hold still!" Laura bent down and moved the base, "Now let go."

Gently, Sam and Donna let go of the panel so that it just rested on top of the base and Laura undid the bolt which held two of the panels together. Where there was once a solid fence, now a gap appeared which was just big enough to scramble through. Parked inside the fence was a small digger. Laura squeezed her way through the gap first and beckoned the others to follow.

Once they were all inside the site, Laura made straight for the office which she unlocked. A smell of dust, bricks and cement made Donna sneeze. "Shh!" hissed Laura.

"What are we looking for?" Sam spoke urgently. "I don't like..." but his words were cut short by the sound of a phone on the desk ringing.

They looked at each other. Laura shook her head and so they waited. One ring, two, three, four, five and then the answerphone message began.

'Wastecom site office. Please leave a message.' Donna held her breath in case whoever it was could sense their presence.

"Paul Glade, here. I seem to have mislaid my keys. Just checking. If they turn up, can you let me know? Thanks." The phone went dead. A smile crept across Laura's face. She dangled the keys in front of the others and giggled.

"Typical. He knows he's lost his keys but he doesn't realise I haven't even been home yet." Donna began to feel afraid of what Laura might be planning to do. "Well, daddy," and she waggled the keys at the phone, "I'll leave your keys for you in the bottom of a drain. Now …" she cast her eyes round the office.

"What are we looking for?" Sam asked.

"A diary, a plan?" Donna suggested hopefully.

"No, this is much more fun," Laura was

studying a series of hooks on the office wall. Seizing a key by its dirty plastic label she ran out of the office. "Come on!"

She raced towards a small digger, parked behind the hut, clambered up into the cab and put the key in the ignition. One twist and it was purring beneath her. She turned back. "Watch me. I'll push the fence over."

Donna grabbed Sam and stepped back into the shadow of the site hut.

"This is not right. We must stop her!" Sam went to run forward but Donna held him back. It was too late. The digger moved slowly forward, its engine rumbling like the purring of a giant cat. Donna and Sam watched, rooted to the spot as the digger stopped by the fence. Laura raised the main arm and used it to push against the fence. The fence wobbled and creaked and with one enormous groan, two of the fence panels slowly toppled over the slope.

Laura switched off the engine and jumped out.

She ran back to the others "See. Now how safe is their stupid site?" But Sam just pointed towards the digger.

"Look!" Laura turned to watch in slow motion as the digger crept forwards.

"Did you put on the brakes?" Donna screamed.

"I think so, I don't know – I mean I'm not sure!"

"What do we do now?"

"Nothing, the rest of the fence will probably stop it and then I can get the keys out!" Laura turned to head back towards the digger.

"You can't! It's too dangerous!" Donna grabbed Laura's arm and pulled her back. Together they watched as the digger trundled slowly forwards. It paused momentarily, the engine growling as it met the fence but the tracks moved relentlessly on and it crashed through the remaining fence and toppled over the edge.

Sam ran forward. The fence panels lay flattened at the foot of the slope. The digger had torn through the trees and bushes, bringing the damp earth down on top of it and it now lay on its side by the stream edge. "We've got to get out of here, now," he called to the other two. "Follow me!" Donna ducked through the tangled remains of the fence and was soon crawling along the narrow ledge at the top of the slope behind Sam. Laura followed. "We can get back to the main path this way," panted Sam.

"Wait for me!" Laura pleaded, her feet sliding on the loose stones as she grabbed hold of a low lying branch to steady her. But the tree roots were not strong enough to hold her weight. Donna heard a piercing scream and turned in time to see Laura tumble head over heels down the slope, in a shower of loose rock, earth and tree roots.

"Sam, stop her!" Donna yelled. Sam turned and straight away swung himself from one tree trunk to another, sometimes sliding, sometimes jumping down the slope until he reached the place where Laura lay. When Donna arrived, Sam was holding

Laura's head in his lap. Her eyes were closed and her leg jutted out from under her body at an uncomfortable angle. Donna bent down and pinched her cheek. Laura groaned.

"It's all right," Donna reassured her. "We'll get help. Sam, you can run faster than me. Go and get my mum and tell her to ring an ambulance."

"Are you sure you'll be ok?" Sam asked. "It's just I don't like to leave you here, alone," and he nodded back towards the digger. Where the slope had collapsed under the weight of the digger, the earth now revealed the unmistakeable shape of a human skeleton.

"Go, Laura's more important than anything else!"

The next ten minutes were like a lifetime. Laura remained still and quiet and whenever Donna turned to look up towards the slope, the grinning skull sent a cold shiver up her spine. From time to time, she bent down and checked Laura's breathing, feeling the warm, damp breath on her cheek. Finally, the distant sound of a siren could be heard. Donna heaved a sigh of relief. "Not long, now, Laura," she whispered.

"Down here." Scrambling down the bank came Sam, followed by two paramedics with a stretcher and behind was Paul Glade and her mum. Sam and Donna got out of the way and watched with Donna's mum as Laura was picked up and strapped safely on the stretcher. Paul Glade turned angrily to face them,

"What happened here? Did you do this?" he stared accusingly at Donna and Sam.

"Not them... my fault..." a groan came from Laura.

"We can find out later what happened. I am sure there is a very reasonable explanation." Donna's mum spoke briskly.

"What about that?" Sam pointed to the skull. Alison turned to where Sam was pointing.

"The police will find out all about that!" she continued. "They are on their way!"

"Is is Annie?" Sam's voice quivered as he stared at the skull. Alison put her arm round his shoulders. "It's ok, Sam," she reassured him. "We'll wait here together until the police arrive while Laura and her father get to hospital." She placed her hand on Paul Glade's arm, "I know it will all be ok. She's a tough kid." Paul nodded. The two paramedics lifted up the stretcher and made their way up the slope to the waiting ambulance.

There was an uneasy silence. "It's not... we didn't mean..." Sam and Donna both spoke at once. Donna's mother held up her hand.

"There will be a time for explanations later." A smile crossed her face. "At least this will slow down Wastecom!"

"But that's what Laura said!"Donna stopped suddenly, "I mean..." her voice tailed away. Sam shuffled his feet uneasily.

"So you do know more about this. Was it just an accident or was it breaking and entering, theft of a vehicle, driving under age? You are both over ten years of age and could be held responsible. Well?" Alison folded her arms and waited for an answer.

Sam shrugged, "Dunno, 'spose so," He scuffed at the earth with his feet and turned back to look at the skull and bones wedged in the damp earth. "It's not her, is it?" he pleaded. Donna shrugged her shoulders.

"Not who?"

"Come on, Sam, we'd better tell the truth."

Sam said nothing but pushed his way through the nettles by the side of the stream. Donna and Alison followed. Sam bent down and carefully removed the branches and ferns. There was a gasp as he smoothed away the leaves and earth to reveal the mosaic.

"It's beautiful!" Alison knelt down by Sam and gazed at the face for what seemed like an age. Then she got up slowly, turned round to face Donna and Sam and stood there, arms on her hips, looking from one to the other, "So just how long have you two known about this?"

"It's a picture of Annie," Sam explained, looking up at Alison, "but I don't want her to be that one…" he pointed towards the skeletal remains. "She can't have died here! This was her home!"

"We'll soon find out," Alison nodded towards the pathway where two police liaison officers were walking towards them, accompanied by three more officers in white forensic suits and masks carrying very large amounts of blue and white tape. The area was now a crime scene.

CHAPTER SEVEN

Tuesday 8ᵗʰ September, 8.45am

The chatter stopped as soon as Donna entered the playground, but not before she had heard the rumours that Laura was dead, had lost her leg or had broken her back and would never walk again. She hung back, hoping to slip in and stand by a teacher. No one would speak to her there, but it was too late.

"Lets' ask Donna – she was there!" The piercing voice of Shelley, Laura's best friend rang out and Donna found herself surrounded by a sea of curious and far from kind faces.

"Well, what happened?" Shelley thrust her fat

face into Donna's and waited, her head tilted to one side.

Donna spoke slowly and softly. "There was an accident and Laura has broken her leg. She's ok but..." her explanation was cut short by Shelley waggling a finger under Donna's chin.

"We know all that but how did it happen? Someone said she was driving a JCB and she'll have to pay thousands!"

"There was an accident. That's all. She fell." Donna repeated the carefully rehearsed lines. The finger poked at her chest again.

"You know more. Tell or else."

"Or else what?" Mr Shah, the duty teacher, alerted by the gang crowding around Donna had come over just in time. "If you are talking about Laura, the Head will tell you all you need to know and if I ever hear a threat like that from you, Shelley Smith, you may find yourself spending your last few months in this school on your own. Now the bell is about to go, line up and let's hear no more."

He motioned for Donna to wait behind.

"If you have any trouble from that lot today, come and let me or the Head know straight away." Then he rang the bell and everyone went and lined up in the required silence. But Donna could feel a hundred eyes piercing her back as she took her place in the line. Sam was late as usual. Donna gritted her teeth and walked into the classroom where the Head teacher waited. There was absolute silence until everyone was sitting down in their place.

Mrs Jarvis went to the front of the room and looked around to make sure that all eyes were on her. "Some of you may have heard about the accident with Laura. I want you all to know that as far as we can tell this was a complete accident." Her eyes caught Donna's who immediately looked down at her desk. "An accident, do you all understand? Apparently she fell and in the fall down that slope that I have told you countless times not to use," she emphasised the 'not'. "She landed awkwardly and broke her leg. Any further investigation is being undertaken by the police and no one else. Until we have heard anything more, the matter is not one to be discussed in school. It is all too easy for people to point the finger and accuse," she paused. "Are you listening Shelley?" The clock ticked loudly in the silent classroom. Donna could see Shelley's chins wobbling indignantly but she nodded all the same. "Good. That is all I have to say on the matter It is now *closed*." She emphasised the word 'closed' and her steely grey eyes swept over every child in the room. "I hope that you will make a card for Laura and send it to her. I am sure we will all miss her." She made her way to the door of the classroom and then turned and paused, "Oh Mrs Jones, I forgot to tell you, there's been a message from Sam's mother. He won't be in till later. Toothache." With a click of her heels, she closed the door behind her.

"You have heard what Mrs Jarvis has said, now let us get on with our learning today," Mrs Jones opened the register and no more was said. Donna got out her reading book and bent her head over it. If she kept a low profile, the excitement would soon pass. And it did, like all things in school. Any talk of Laura was soon eclipsed by Jason, who got himself locked in the toilet and couldn't get out. He was missing from assembly time until break time. Eventually when he was found, he had to be rescued by the caretaker who had to dismantle the whole toilet cubicle.

Sam did not appear all day and it was during the late afternoon, when the class were writing up their account of Henry the Eighth's marriages that a phone call came through. "Donna, your mother is here. You are to go up to the office. Take your things. You need to go now." Donna put her book into her tray and slipped out of the room to a sigh of envy. Anything was better than writing and to be able to leave early without any withering comment about missing important learning time from Mrs Jones meant it must be very important.

Alison was waiting there. "I've signed you out. We have a meeting, at the police station," she added. Donna climbed into the front of the car and they travelled in silence with Donna repeating over and over to herself exactly what she would say. When they reached the station, they were ushered into a small room furnished with sofas and armchairs and they waited. Sam, his mouth swollen from the dentist, came in next, followed by his mother, who kept smoothing back her grey hair and looking anxiously round her. Then Paul Glade arrived, pushing a wheelchair with a very glum Laura in it, her leg encased in plaster and sticking out in front of her. Everyone looked embarrassedly around the room at the floor, chairs, even the backs of their own hands, anywhere rather than at each other.

The silence was broken by the entry of two police officers; one Donna recognised as the lady who came to school to talk to them from time to time. She smiled as she sat down and got out a small notebook. "We are just waiting for the duty sergeant and the Area Manager of Wastecom." Donna noticed Paul Glade jump at the mention of Wastecom, but still said nothing although he did straighten his tie and bend down to rub off a speck of mud from his shiny, black shoes.

A few more agonising seconds passed and then the door swung open again and in walked the sergeant and a very pretty red haired woman in a silver grey suit and the highest heeled shoes Donna had ever seen. Paul Glade immediately sat up and straightened his tie again. "Right a few introductions all round and then we need answers to some questions before Ms Challis of Wastecom makes up her mind whether to press charges," the duty sergeant explained.

"Challis?" Donna looked up to see Paul Glade turning red and squirming in his seat, "but I thought you were a..."

"A man? That is what everyone thinks. As you can see I am not, Mister Glade but let us get on with the business in hand before we discuss my gender any further," and she folded her hands over her elegantly crossed legs. The sergeant looked round at all of them in turn and then cleared his throat.

"As I was saying, a few introductions," but he was interrupted again.

"It's my fault – everything. Please don't blame Sam and Donna, it's all my fault." Laura spoke quietly and then stopped. She looked at Paul Glade. "I really am sorry dad. But it seemed like a good idea at the time." She turned her head to look at Donna. "And I'm sorry for everything I've done. I've been mean and cruel to everyone!" and she began to cry softly.

AD 176 at night

The flood waters were rising fast. The animals had long since been moved to higher ground, but still Aurea waited. It had been five years since Luca had left for the life of a legionnaire. The letters had been few and far between, but Luca was a success and was now expected back any time in the town. Aurea had spent those years studying and helping Luca's mother, who had never been happy since his departure, always fearing the worst. Aurea had refused to go with the family and now stayed behind with Julia, who could not leave the baby she had brought up as her own. Aurea would never forgive herself if Luca should return to find an empty house.

The Churn was a small river, never known to flood so Aurea felt quite safe inside the villa. But like a slow moving tide of destruction, the waters were moving ever closer to the house as the rain continued to pour from leaden skies. Aurea and Julia stood at the window and watched, helpless as the waters rose steadily to engulf the outhouses and the mud bricks collapsed under the force and weight of the water. Night fell but still the rain continued to fall.

As the light of a cold, wet dawn broke, Aurea felt the house shake and quiver. She woke and leaned out of the window. A wall of water with trees and dead animals was surging towards her. Soon the villa would be surrounded; an island in the middle of the water with no way out. It was too late now to leave and Luca would never risk coming here, even if he was back in Corinium. Julia and Aurea clung to each other and waited for a certain death.

AND THEN...

Tuesday September 8th, 4.30pm

The drive home was conducted in silence. Laura, stretched out with her leg resting on the back seat, pretended to study the contours of the plaster. She was relieved that she had taken full responsibility for the accident and that she'd apologised to Donna for her spitefulness. But both Sam and Donna had confessed their part too which made it all easier. She wondered if Shelley would have been so honest. She liked Donna and the way she had stayed with her and not run off. But at least there were to be no charges. Although her father's tight lipped, "We will discuss this further at home," meant there were more interrogations to come.

The car pulled up and stopped in the driveway. Sarah opened the front door and waved. Laura waited as her father lifted her out of the back seat and helped her into the wheel chair. Sarah wheeled her into the lounge, which had been re arranged with a space for her chair and a footstool with her favourite books, games and her phone placed on a small table exactly within her reach.

It was Sarah who helped her get settled. "Jamie is staying over with his friends so there's just us three. Promise you will tell me if there is anything else that you need. I want to make sure you have everything within reach." Sarah plumped up some cushions and tucked them behind Laura's back, then stood back and smiled.

"Stop fussing, Sarah, this young lady has given us the run around for far too long. I think we all deserve a few more explanations, all this rubbish about stopping Wastecom." He glared at Laura.

"Since when did you become an eco warrior like that Alison woman, or has everyone gone eco mad!?"

"Paul, please, let me say something," Sarah sat down next to Laura and put her cool hand on Laura's. "Look I know you don't like me but I love your dad and he loves me. I am trying to make a home for you and Jamie and the new baby when it arrives. All I want is for you to try to accept me and to work with me." She paused. "But there are times when I will be tough on you. But that's because I care and want you to grow up as someone that your mum would have been proud of. If I don't do that I will have failed you, your dad and your mum's memory. I can't replace your mum, but perhaps I can be a second-best mum and you can help me when the baby arrives – and I can help you whenever you need a friend to help you out." There was another pause. "Now can we try, again?" Laura nodded and smiled.

"Does that mean I won't be sent away to

school?" Laura shot a glance at her father but it was Sarah who spoke first.

"No, not while I am here unless we all agree it is for the best. Who knows, you might one day want to go to sport college or drama school but that is for the future."

"But any messing us around and you will be grounded, do you understand?" And whatever was going on between you and Donna, it stops now. She seems like a good kid – better than some friends you have!" Paul had to have the last word and for once Laura let him. Perhaps in time, she could even invite Donna to tea or to stop over.

Tuesday September 8th, 4.40pm

Alison kicked off her shoes and flung herself down on the sofa. "Whatever you kids planned, it worked! Wastecom and that scheming Paul Glade are defeated. I loved seeing the look on his face when that woman Challis as good as blamed him for the whole thing – telling him to take more notice of 'community feelings'. " Donna sat down on the armchair and let Romeo climb on her lap where he sat contentedly washing his paws, in anticipation of his next meal.

"Fancy Wastecom going green," Alison went on, enjoying remembering Challis's words, which she repeated, savouring every syllable. "So it has been decided that we will not press charges, but use the opportunity to move the site to the new industrial complex on the other side of the town." She punched at the air. "We can make a bigger depot there and so create more jobs as well as build a facility that has a zero carbon footprint. It will be the flagship for Wastecom's new philosophy!" She smiled again at the memory. " And I bet Paul Glade's company won't have a part to play."

Alison turned back to Donna, "But you must promise me not to meddle in these sorts of things again. There are ways of helping, but that does not mean taking the law into your own hands."

"I did it for Sam, "Donna spoke quietly. "He didn't want anything to happen to the mosaic. He wanted everything to stay as it is. I don't care about your campaigns; I'm fed up with them. Why can't we be ordinary, like everyone else?" Donna stood up suddenly, sending Romeo to the floor where he immediately climbed back to take her place in the armchair. "I'm going to my room."

"Don't go, love, come back and tell me what's wrong." Alison patted the cushion next to her. Donna sat down next to her mother and drew her knees up to her chin. "Now tell your old mum what's wrong? And what do you mean by being 'ordinary'?"

"Just that, you're always so busy doing things. Sometimes, can I have a friend for tea? Or even a sleepover? And when can we spend my birthday money? All you ever do is your campaigns." She stopped. It was Alison who eventually broke the silence.

"You're right, things do have to change," she admitted. "I've got my old job back in the library, just four mornings a week so I won't have time for more than one campaign, but don't ever expect me not to do something."

"I don't," replied Donna.

"But I don't see why we can't have a girly day out shopping from time to time. There's a lovely place for ethnic clothing at the top of the market. It's all eco friendly and very reasonable. And I am sure we can invite a few friends here from time to time. Money won't be so tight now I've got a job. What about that for a start?"

Donna nodded. "Can we go this Saturday? The 'welcome back' disco is next week and I'd like to buy something to wear."

"Agreed. But there is another thing. What was happening with you and that girl Laura? Were you being bullied?"

Donna nodded. "Why didn't you say something to me or to your teacher?" Donna shrugged.

"It might have made things worse and we were told in year four that we had to be kind to her because her mum died."

"That was in year four! No one has the right to make anyone else unhappy just because they've had a rough time. Now promise me you will never ever do that again. Promise?"

"I promise."

"Now that's settled, why don't we celebrate with a curry? I'll ring for a take away. Your usual? Alison went towards the hall, "And I can just see you in some of those lovely floaty cotton clothes from Nepal. No sweat shop produced those."

But Donna had no intention of wearing such things, particularly as right next door to 'The Real Clothing Company' was a shop that specialised in the latest fashion. Donna was certain she could easily slip away from her mother, particularly if she could leave Tom and her mother having a coffee. Then she could buy exactly what she wanted. She reached for the remote control and switched on

MTV, imagining how good new silver dolphin ear rings, a glittery top with some new black trousers and boots would look.

Saturday December 15th, 11.00am

Donna pushed Sam through the entrance of the museum and went straight to the desk. "We're here to see Dr Maisie Vine," she held out a letter for the museum attendant to read.

"Wait here," the attendant pressed a button. "Sam Maloney and a friend are here to see you." Donna looked around and pointed at a notice, 'Exciting new excavations to begin alongside the River Churn, sponsored by Wastecom. See the latest discoveries as they happen in our new interactive exhibition.'

"So these are my two amateur archaeologists." Donna and Sam turned to see Dr Vine, smiling warmly, "Come this way." She led the children to the Roman section and up a flight of stairs. In the centre of the floor was a glass cabinet, surrounded by a backdrop showing a villa and men and women in Roman clothes and an enormous photograph of the mosaic that Sam had found of the girl's face. In an open stone coffin lay the skeleton and next to it on a stand covered in purple velvet was the snake bracelet. Donna peered at a card and nudged Sam as she read, 'Found along side the River Churn on the site of a villa by Sam Maloney.'

The next card, placed by the coffin read, 'Male skeleton, approximately 30 years of age found on the site of the same villa from approximately 450 AD '.

"How can you be sure it's not a young girl?" Sam asked, his nose pressed so close to the glass case that his breath condensed on the surface.

"The bones of the pelvis show it was a male and the age is indicated by the condition and age of the teeth," Dr. Vine spoke authoritatively. "An initial examination showed us that the teeth were quite worn down and chipped. Teeth got chipped by stones in the corn. No dentists in those days. We know that sometimes when these villas were left derelict, they were rebuilt and inhabited later on by poorer people. I expect this is what happened here."

"So it couldn't have been that girl, there?" Sam pointed at the photo of the mosaic.

"I doubt it," Dr Vine smiled. "The villa and the style of the mosaics is dated from the second century AD, but the skeleton is definitely later! Also poor people didn't have mosaics done. No, this young girl looks every bit a Roman dignitary; a wealthy family lived in that villa. Probably the original family moved elsewhere and the villa was left to fall into ruins. No estate agents to sell them on in those days!"

There was silence as each individual stared at the exhibits, lost in their own thoughts.

"The mosaics really are outstanding," Dr. Vine

continued, "and with Wastecom's very generous sponsorship, we will be able to reconstruct it all here in the museum. You are welcome to come back any time and see the progress of work. Your discovery is one of the most important things we have ever found in the area!"

"Do you think this mosaic could be Annie?" Sam looked up expectantly.

"Well 'Annie' is not a common Roman name."

"What about the skeleton?"

"It's definitely a man! So perhaps that story in the school should be about an 'Arnold', not an 'Annie'. Anyway, there's no such things as ghosts, certainly not in schools with you lot rampaging around! Now I must get back to my work." She turned and left the children quietly looking at the exhibits.

"Sam, can I ask you a question?" Donna whispered.

"What?" grunted Sam, still staring at the skeleton.

"Do you still believe in the story of Annie?"

Sam thought for a moment, "Not really, there's more likely to be aliens on the school field!"

"Aliens?"

"Yeah – there's a big burnt patch in a circle – that must have been aliens!"

"Sam, that was caused by the Round Table bonfire way back in November!"

"Oh…" Sam continued to look at girl's face. "Do you think she was happy?"

"No one is ever completely happy or sad," Donna spoke in a hushed voice, "There's good and bad in everything, my granddad says, but..." she paused. "I hope so."

They both remained there deep in their own thoughts for a few minutes before Donna broke the spell. "Come on, I've got money for some chips."

As they went back down the steps, Donna turned once more to look at the face of the young girl in the mosaic. As the eyes of the present looked at the eyes of the past, an echo crossed the centuries and Donna spoke with assurance, "You know, Sam, I reckon she was very happy."

AD 176, morning

The cold grey light of a watery dawn crept over the flooded woodland and meadows where Aurea and Luca had played as children. The villa stood as if marooned, like an island surrounded by sea. As Aurea stood up and went over towards the open upstairs window, she was certain she could hear something.

Someone was approaching carefully through the shallower flood waters at the front of the house. Although Aurea could not see the face, she recognised the voice. "Aurea, come quickly the water is getting higher." She ran over to Julia and shook her .

"Wake up , it is Luca. He has returned."

Together they ran down the stairs and waded

across the flooded mosaic floor of the villa. Their footsteps splashed and covered over the gentle sound of something metal, falling to the floor. Outside, Luca was waiting with two horses. Aurea looked up into the face of a young man, not the child she remembered but it was still Luca. Together they helped Julia to mount the smaller horse, then Luca pulled Aurea up behind him and with a flick of the reins, he led the way to safety. It was not until they had reached higher land and stopped that Aurea noticed her bracelet was missing. In her haste to get away, it must have fallen off somewhere.

It was several days later that Aurea and Luca returned. Where the house had stood was a pile of rubble. The foundations could not hold up against the floodwaters. "But we will never find my bracelet now," Aurea cried.

"I will buy you another one, far finer when we build our new house," Luca laughed, "but not here, this is poor farmland and if the river has flooded once, it can happen again. I have found land at a place called 'Kingscote'. That is where we will build a new home," and together they turned and left the ruins to the wind and the weather.

Wednesday 21st December, 8.30pm

The sounds of the last track at the disco faded away and Laura, Shelley and Sam helped Mrs Jarvis usher the younger children outside to where their parents were waiting in the dark night air. Donna and Laura carried the money from the tuck shop into the school office. Mr Shah was busy counting it out. "Oh Donna, can you run down the corridor and put these stamps away in my cupboard, unless it's too dark and scary!" he added his eyes twinkling.

"It's not scary – besides, Laura will come with me!"

"What about Annie?"

"But Mr Shah, don't you realise, there's no such things as ghosts?" they chorused as they ran off.

It was much later when all of the children had gone home, the disco had been dismantled and driven away and Paul Glade had collected his 'gang of four' as he called them to take Laura, Sam, Donna and Shelley for a late evening burger that Mrs Jarvis set the alarm and closed the door behind her. It had been a long evening and she shivered as she went out into the cold night air. A mist was forming over the school field and as she looked up at the bell tower, the mist wreathed around it like a white, sinuous arm. She shivered again, 'You're getting as bad as the children,' she told herself, 'Don't you realise there's no such thing as ghosts!'

THE END

NOTES

Information on items in italics can be found in the Corinium Museum in Cirencester or on their website at **http://www.cotswold.gov.uk** and follow the link to the museum pages.

Chapter one

Until the second century, Romans could abandon an unwanted child. It was certain to die of cold or hunger unless someone took it to care for as their own. Aurea knows that Gaius would not be able to this.

Twenty thousand Sestertii each year (about £500) was considered just enough for a Roman citizen to live comfortably in Rome at this time.

Other coins at the time were as follows;

1 gold Aureus= 25 silver Denarii

1 Denarius = 4 bronze Sestertii

1 Sestertii = 2 bronze Dupandii

1 As= 2 copper Semis

Chapter 2

Reddish brown pottery called Samian ware was common in Corinium during the early Roman era, particularly in the first century AD when an army was stationed there.

A long woollen hooded cloak known as a Birrus Britannicus was worn over the tunic to keep warm.

The Triclinium or dining room usually contained three couches and a table in the centre.

The Dobunni tribe were the original inhabitants of the area around Cirencester. They were farmers who grew wheat and barley and kept cattle, sheep and pigs.

Slaves were often educated, treated well and in the second century AD, at least a fifth could be given their freedom.

A modest citizen would have at least 8 slaves whilst the Imperial house would have thousands, many of whom were educated well enough to be able to do the tasks required of them.

Chapter 3

The Verulamium gate was built close to where Beeches Road is today and would be the closest gate to the villa in the story.

Corinium was an important wool town for many centuries. The fleece was carded between spikes to make the strands of fibre lie in the same direction. Then the roll of carded wool was spun before being woven into cloth. Wool could be woven with silk to create cloth.

Chapter 4

Triclinium – see chapter 2

Writing was first practiced on a wax tablet with a stylus. The stylus was usually pointed at one end to make the marks. The other end was flat to smooth the wax again. A pen could be made from a quill from a feather and dipped into ink. A wax tablet was found in a waterlogged part of Cirencester.

The walls were painted in bight colours with patterns on them. The mosaic floors were laid on top of the hypocaust heating system. The patterns, shapes and pictures varied but were all made up of small blocks called 'tesserae'.

The mosaic of hunting dogs and the mosaic of the four seasons were found in the same house and date to this time.

Chapter 5

The town was laid out with roads and alleyways in straight lines and right angles. The forum was a central meeting place. The pavement that they follow was a mosaic in red, black and silver grey in the shape of flowers with a knotted design intertwined. The pavement was found in Victoria Road, Cirencester.

Saturnalia was a mid winter festival.